The faster you run, the keener the hunter

"And right now there isn't anything I wouldn't do to have you," Adam told her thickly. "All the time I've been away I've been thinking about you, wanting you, and I don't like it!"

"No," Brooke shot back at him. "You treat women like disposable hankies—use them and discard them—just because wealthy Susan Delaney once refused to dance with you."

"Damn you for that, Brooke," Adam swore hoarsely, and then his mouth was on hers, fiercely demanding, making her want to match the fury of his embrace. "What do you want?" he demanded savagely as he released her. "To be the only one?"

Yes, her heart cried with furious intensity as she fought to keep her face controlled. "I never hope for the impossible," she said dryly.

Books by Penny Jordan

HARLEQUIN PRESENTS

These books may be available at your local bookseller.

Don't miss any of our special offers. Write to us at the following address for information on our newest releases.

Harlequin Reader Service
P.O. Box 52040, Phoenix, AZ 85072-2040
Canadian address: P.O. Box 2800, Postal Station A,
5170 Yonge St., Willowdale, Ont. M2N 6J3

PENNY JORDAN

the only one

Harlequin Books

TORONTO • NEW YORK • LONDON
AMSTERDAM • PARIS • SYDNEY • HAMBURG
STOCKHOLM • ATHENS • TOKYO • MILAN

Harlequin Presents first edition May 1985
ISBN 0-373-10785-4

Original hardcover edition published in 1984
by Mills & Boon Limited

Printed in U.S.A.

CHAPTER ONE

SHE hadn't wanted to come to this party, and now that she was here, it was proving every bit as dreadful as she had envisaged, Brooke thought, almost instantly mocking herself for the immaturity of the thought. She was twenty-six for heaven's sake, not sixteen. A wry grimace firmed the soft contours of her full mouth and across the width of the generously proportioned drawing room a man engaged in conversation with his companion caught the faint movement and watched her, slate grey eyes narrowing assessingly.

She had always known she wouldn't be able to keep Abbot's Meade, Brooke acknowledged, absently twirling her wine glass by its stem, her glance drifting over the view afforded by the drawing-room window. The view outside was as familiar to her as her own features; she knew exactly how many tall lime trees went to make up the lined drive that led from the front gates to the front of the house, just as she knew every inch of the grounds in which they stood. Abbot's Meade had been in her family since the fifteenth century and her uncle had been the last male Meade left.

Ancestor worship was always something she had faintly despised, but there was something sad, almost painfully so, about having to come face to face with the fact that they had reached the end of an era.

Even during her uncle's lifetime there had been insufficient funds to keep the estate going. Bits had gradually been sold off and eventually even the house itself had had to be mortgaged, and now that her uncle was gone, as her solicitor had said, there was nothing to be gained from hanging on any longer. And she had agreed with him. Even so . . . She was unaware of the faintly sardonic twist to her mouth as she glanced round the room, or that her contempt had been witnessed. The house had eventually been sold to a large corporation who intended to turn it into their headquarters. This party was being thrown to celebrate their new acquisition. Brooke hadn't wanted to attend, even though she had been invited, but Sam Brockbank, her solicitor, had persuaded her. 'Don't forget, you're going to be living practically on their doorstep,' he had reminded her. 'There's no point in antagonising them, Brooke.'

That much was true. Although the house, the Dower House in which she had lived as a child with her parents, and the parkland had been sold, she had retained the rights to the small cottage just by the gates which had once been the lodgekeeper's home. The cottage had its own garden and its own gate on to the main road which made her independent of the main house, but it would be difficult to remember that she no longer had the right to walk through that small garden into the main park, or to saddle up a horse from the stable and ride through it, as she had done in the past. Mentally mocking herself Brooke studied the occupants of the rooms. In the main, business-suited men with matching wives, they all exhibited the same glossy success-orientated sheen; all except one man. Frowning Brooke fought not to let her glance slide away as her own scrutiny was returned, a thousand times more assessingly.

Whoever he was this man plainly wasn't afraid of flouting conventions.

Tall, with carefully schooled black hair that looked as though it preferred to be unruly he had a face that suggested it might have been carved out of granite—or marble, Brooke corrected herself noting with a small shock of surprise, the almost too-perfect symmetry of bones and flesh as she caught a glimpse of his profile. Without the hard muscled strength his dinner suit did little to conceal he might almost have been *too* good looking she reflected, too engrossed in her own thoughts and conclusions to avoid the sudden trap of steely grey eyes as they meshed with hers and held her an unwilling prisoner.

Years ago Brooke had learned to be skilled in avoiding unwanted confrontations with the opposite sex. At five foot ten with a mane of dark red hair, long long legs and a well curved body she was used to dealing with a variety of unwanted come-ons from over-assertive males, including the accusation that by returning their scrutiny she was implicitly inviting their advances.

By some odd meshing of fate Brooke had inherited not her mother's pretty, fair, Meade looks, nor her father's darker French ones, but those of a long-ago Scots ancestor, which had resulted in a fine Celtic bone structure to match her red hair and golden-green eyes.

As a teenager she had been gawky and too thin; she had also been reasonably popular with her own sex, but in her late teens when she had flowered into womanhood she had discovered that her popularity decreased in direct ratio to her blossoming femininity.

'You're becoming too sexy,' one girl had told

her bluntly when she had asked why she was no longer included in invitations. 'You're just too much competition for the rest of us, Brooke.'

It had been shortly after that that her parents were killed in a freak car ferry accident—eight years ago now, and in those eight years she had learned to wear her unwanted mantle of 'sexiness' as best she could.

Grim humour etched a smile across her face. 'Sexy'—if only they knew—her sexual experience was limited to the teenage fumblings she had indulged in until loneliness had driven her into her protective shell. Why was she feeling so sorry for herself, she derided herself mockingly. She was celibate by choice, not circumstance. There had been plenty of opportunities for her to indulge herself in sexual adventurings had she wanted to do so, but a certain fastidiousness made her hold back. She wasn't foolish enough to believe in the myth of love and the perfect one and only—that was for adolescents; nor had she any moral reservations; men felt perfectly free to indulge in as many sexual encounters as they wished—she only needed to think of the many married men of her acquaintance who had approached her for dates if she needed proof of that—so why shouldn't women? No, it was something other than that that held her aloof; something that had been born about the same time as she lost her friends and heard her mother saying almost reverently, 'Brooke, you're going to be the most stunningly beautiful woman. . . .'

Physical beauty was all very well in its way, but it had its drawbacks. Unacknowledged, but lying at the back of her mind, was the knowledge that she wanted a man who would look beyond the façade of her beauty; a man who would want to know *her* . . . not just her face and figure.

She glanced down at her glass. Her wine had run out along with her patience with this party. She grimaced faintly again. Time she was making a move.

Sam, her solicitor, had been disapproving because she wanted to know so little about the people buying Abbot's Meade, and she hadn't had the energy to explain to him that the less she knew the more easy it was to shut herself off from the pain of losing the place. As always Brooke was half-amused by her own intensity of feeling, the logical, French side of her nature mocking her sentimentality about a few acres of land and a house that common sense said she could never hope to hold on to or preserve as it should be preserved. During the last few years of his life she had helped nurse her uncle and had lived here at Abbot's Meade with him, giving up her secretarial job in London.

The late autumn afternoon was fast fading into dusk. She had every excuse to leave. It was a half-mile walk down to her cottage; she had no car, and the drive wasn't illuminated. That would soon be changed, she reflected grimly. The new owners planned to put in lighting; perhaps they'd cut down the limes to make way for the lamp posts, was her sardonic thought as she started to make her way with lazy ease towards the door. With luck Sam wouldn't notice she had gone until it was too late. Almost a head taller than the majority of the other women in the room, her tailored black suit a perfect foil for her red hair Brooke was unaware of how many pairs of eyes charted her progress, many of them with envy; some of them with sexual appraisal, and one pair in particular with sharp curiosity.

'Adam, you aren't listening to me. . . .'

Dark eyebrows rose as Adam Henderson turned towards his companion, cold grey eyes masking his thoughts. 'Sorry Bill,' he apologised, 'my mind was on other things.' A cool glance in the direction of the tall redhead heading for the door made Bill Edwards frown. As head of Hart Industries, Adam had no equal; he had built up his empire from the most humble of beginnings; his father had died when he was a child and his mother had worked as a cleaner to support and educate him, and Bill, who was ex-Eton and the Guards, had nothing but admiration for him; but he knew that look in Adam's eyes and his heart sank. When Adam embarked on the chase and inevitable capture of some hapless member of the female sex it always resulted in a sudden charge of energy that left the rest of his executive staff drained and exhausted.

The last time Bill had seen him look like that had been in New York. Adam had ended up adding a developing maintenance company to his building empire and yet another scalp to his belt.

'Who is she?' Adam asked him softly, not bothering to waste any time on pointless preliminaries. All his life he had seen a goal and worked punishingly towards it, once reaching it abandoning the pursuit in favour of something else, and at thirty-six he didn't see why he should change now.

'Brooke Beauclere, you bought this place from her.' Bill told him dryly. He made it his business to always have these sort of facts at his finger-tips—that was how he kept his job as one of the highest paid executive directors in the country. If there was one thing Adam would not tolerate it was complacent, sloppy staff. That was why his companies won so many prestigious building contracts; why he could now pick and choose those contracts; because any architect who worked alongside a Henderson company knew that the specifications would be fulfilled right down to the last nail. And Adam believed in maintaining that same quality throughout every aspect of his business.

'I did?' The dark eyebrows lifted again. 'She doesn't look too pleased about it. How much did we pay?'

'Just under half a million, but the place was heavily mortgaged, and I believe she's donated most of the rest of the money to the local children's hospital.'

'Ah, one of the old brigade; an old name, a crumbling mansion and a set of values her ancestors would have laughed to scorn—this place was never acquired through genteel manners and do-goodiness. Still, with that face and body she can always raise another half a million—perhaps more.'

The cynical comment was too much in keeping with his boss's nature for Bill to question it. One of that same 'old brigade', Adam had just derided, he knew when to keep his mouth closed. While it wouldn't be entirely true to say that Adam had a chip on his shoulder, there was an awareness in him that in some circles he was accepted very much on sufferance because of his working-class origins, and Bill knew that it goaded him.

Perhaps it had something to do with the fact that his mother had worked as a cleaner in the

Manor House of the small Yorkshire village where Adam had grown up. He certainly kept his feelings on the subject well hidden, but there were occasions, like now, when he allowed them to surface. Bill had a vivid memory of his own interview with Adam and the latter's faintly derogatory remarks about ex-public schoolboys playing their way through life. When he had explained that an uncle had paid for his education, Adam had altered his attitude slightly.

'What does she do?' Adam asked without taking his eyes off her tall, fluid body.

'Nothing, she nursed her uncle up until his death, and before that apparently worked in the city as a secretary.'

'Umm . . . was she a good one?'

'So it seems. She's fluent in several foreign languages—especially French. Her father was French.'

On her way to the door Brooke had been stopped by her solicitor, who insisted on appropriating another glass of warm white wine for her.

'Surely you're not leaving already Brooke?' he complained. 'I wanted to talk to you about this donation to the hospital.'

'Sam, I'm not going to change my mind,' she told him positively. 'They need that money far more than I do. I've got the Lodge,' she persisted, when he would have interrupted, 'and I have the ability to earn my own living. What more do I need?'

'A job,' he told her wryly. 'My dear girl, have you thought yet? Where are you going to find a job round here? Abbot's Meade is a small country town, there's nothing here for a woman like you. . . .'

'Apart from my roots,' she reminded him equally wryly. 'Sam, when are you going to accept that I don't want a glamorous high life. I'm quite content to stay here. . . .'

'Maybe now,' he agreed, 'but what about in five years' time? Surely you don't intend to stay single all your life?'

'And London is a better hunting ground for husbands?' she mocked him. 'Or perhaps you were thinking that if I didn't make the donation to the hospital I could buy myself one, after all it wouldn't be the first time that had happened in this family; an old name in exchange for new money.'

Someone else claimed his attention and as she watched her solicitor turn away Brooke eyed a nearby rubber plant and then looked distastefully into her glass of unappealing wine, unaware that she was being observed.

She had just finished pouring the contents of her glass into the peat when she saw him.

At close quarters he was even more magnetising than he had seemed across the width of the room. Slate grey eyes appraised her thoughtfully, the smile that touched his mouth a combination of insolence and experience. She disliked him on sight, Brooke acknowledged, repressing the small shiver of response quivering through her—an unusual reaction for her, and one she was careful to conceal from him, like a quarry suddenly scenting its hunter.

'Why did you do that?' He gestured towards her empty glass, his smile assured and knowing—knowing the effect his particular brand of intense masculinity must have on her sex, Brooke thought, covertly studying him. Perhaps it was time someone gave his massive ego a jolt. Smiling with saccharine sweetness she responded. 'I'm a reformed alcoholic forbidden to touch spirits or wine.'

For a moment he seemed taken aback and then amusement glinted in the depths of his eyes, no longer cold, but warmly slumberous, their expression flashing warning signals to Brooke's brain.

'Umm ... and what could drive a beautiful woman like you to seek refuge in drink, I wonder?'

'Oh, all the usual things,' Brooke responded nastily, 'but most particularly men who look at me as though they're sizing me up for their next meal.'

'That frightens you?' If anything he looked even more amused.

Brooke snapped her teeth together and spoke through them. 'No, it offends me—just as it would offend you if the boot were on the other foot.' When he continued to look amused, she added coolly. 'I can see that you aren't convinced, but believe me if you had to fend off every member of the female sex who found you attractive and who thought that that gave her the right to make a play for you, you'd soon realise how offensive it can be.'

'Really? I've always found a simple "No thanks" perfectly adequate.' He flashed white teeth in a faintly cruel smile, and Brooke found herself wondering cattily who had done his dental work. If it wasn't for that slight chip in one of them she might almost have believed they had been falsely enamelled.

'Then *I'm* saying "No thanks" to you right now,' she told him recklessly, suddenly searingly angry without really knowing why she should be.

She glanced over her shoulder, half expecting to see an irate wife bearing down on them. Why was it that women always acquitted their erring husbands of the blame? She had received more frosty looks from her own sex than she could count, and if they had but known it her interest in their dull husbands had been less than nil.

'Are you now?' The deep voice was unexpectedly soft, shooting warning flares along Brooke's nerve endings. 'I wasn't aware that you'd been asked.'

There were several responses she could have made. She could have pointed out that the way he was looking at her was invitation enough, but she was too stunned to speak, and he used his initiative relentlessly watching her colour change and deepen as she fought against her growing anger.

'When you're angry your eyes change from green to gold,' he remarked softly. 'Did you know that? What are you doing here? You look as out of place as a goldfish in a village pond.'

'If that was meant to be a compliment you can keep it,' she told him crisply, spoiling it by adding, 'anyway in Japan goldfish do inhabit the village pond.'

'And women know their rightful place,' he tormented her, 'so what conclusions are we to draw from that?'

'I haven't the faintest idea.' Her expression was disdainfully uninterested. She glanced at her watch, a twenty-first present from her uncle and bought in the days before she discovered the state of his financial affairs. It was a gold Piaget and she treasured it more because he had given it to her than because of its value.

The grey eyes watching her had suddenly

darkened, flashing storm signals that startled her. 'A present from a grateful admirer?'

His voice was taunting, his expression one she was familiar with on male faces. So he thought the watch had been given to her by a lover; well let him.

Pinning a false smile to her lips she responded coolly, 'Of course.... And now if you'll excuse me....'

'You're leaving? Why?'

His arrogance infuriated her afresh. What business of his was it if she chose to leave?

'Because I'm bored,' she told him sweetly.

'The company not good enough for you? Perhaps there isn't anyone here wealthy enough to supply you with another of these?' His fingers circled her wrist just below her watch, stroking the fragile bones, sensitising her flesh in a way that Brooke couldn't believe possible. She was torn between wanting to tug her wrist away, and giving way to the melting sensation of pleasure spreading up her arm, making her finger-tips tingle. The intensity of her response startled her to the point of not being able to correlate her thoughts, and the rough drawl of his voice broke the physical spell momentarily binding her to him as he continued mockingly, 'But I'm sure they'd be willing to give you other if less valuable baubles in return for some of your time....'

'Only my time?' Inwardly Brooke was seething, but she hid it well, as she had grown used to doing.

'Or perhaps you're playing for higher stakes,' the soft drawl continued. 'One large item is so much more worthwhile than several cheaper ones, and easier to earn,' he added cynically.

It wasn't the first time Brooke had come up against such an attitude, and she doubted that it would be the last. By some trick of fate the delineation of her facial features was such that she possessed a slumberous, almost sensual quality that men automatically assumed meant that she was sexually available. That, in a way, she could understand and excuse, but what she couldn't forgive was their immediate reaction that being available meant she could be bought—and by the highest bidder. This man it seemed was no different from the rest, and despite the fact that he lacked the smooth polish of many of the other men in the room with him, he did possess all the discreet trappings of wealth. Brooke's mouth tightened. He was an arrogant, over-confident male who seemed to think he could just reach out and take whatever he wanted from life. Perhaps it was time someone taught him a lesson.

'Meaning?' Brooke queried, mentally holding her breath.

'Meaning,' came the audacious response, 'that I'm in a position to provide the one large item.' A lazy smile accompanied the lightly spoken words, his expression saying that this conversation was really unnecessary, as the result was already a foregone conclusion. For one moment Brooke was tempted to blast him with the full force of her wrath, but caution, and a searing need to humiliate him as he had just humiliated her, intervened. How dare he imagine that she was his simply for the buying; that she would ever dream of agreeing to the sort of sordid bargain he had just suggested? Her quick brain agilely sifting through their conversation, Brooke thought she had found a way to make sure he would never again look at a woman with the same contemptuous confidence with which he had just smiled at her.

'Which do you prefer,' she was asked as she remained silent, 'cash or kind?' When she turned shocked gold eyes towards cold grey ones, Adam shrugged and said easily, 'I do prefer to get these annoying details sorted out beforehand, don't you? It makes life easier all round.'

'You prefer paying for your sex?' Brooke asked him, hardly able to believe she was having this conversation.

The broad dinner-suited shoulders shrugged. 'I believe in an honest exchange of commodities—yes, and women always intend men to pay in one way or the other don't they?' He added less pleasantly, 'It's just that the majority of them prefer their payment in emotional coin—far more damaging to the pocket in the long run.'

'Meaning?' Again Brooke put the brief question.

'Meaning that I'm not in the market for emotional involvement,' Adam told her coolly. 'I always like to make that clear right from the start.'

'Very wise of you, I'm sure.' Brooke hid her surprise under a veil of indifference. From his attitude she wasn't the first woman he had approached in this way, by a long chalk. How had the others reacted? Or was this the first time he had mistaken his quarry? Brooke wasn't blind to the fault of her sex; there were women, and she knew plenty of them, who would be quite happy to accept his offer—providing it was more prettily packaged to be sure, and yet one look at him had been sufficient for her to know that he possessed a sexual magnetism that few women would be able to resist, and that they would want him for himself alone.

'So, do we have a bargain?'

Caution warned her to refuse—to stop the game while she still could, but a deep inner burning anger overruled caution and she heard herself saying calmly, 'Yes, I believe we do.'

'So . . . tonight, then?'

He didn't waste much time, Brooke reflected, concealing her consternation. 'Very well, tonight. I live in the Lodge at the end of the drive.'

'I'll be there at ten.'

No pretence of wining and dining her first, Brooke noted, one half of her applauding his cynical down-to-earth attitude while the other half was horrified, cringing away from the implications of his comment. Obviously he was a man well used to getting what he wanted, but tonight she was going to blast a hole into that immense self-conceit which she told herself a little fancifully was going to be not just a blow for herself, but for the whole of womankind—or at least that part of it young and attractive enough to catch the eye of Mr——? She frowned, realising that she didn't even know his name, subduing the hysterical bubbles of laughter rising up inside her, at the thought that she had verbally committed herself to going to bed with a man whose name she didn't even know, and who didn't know hers.

'I'm Brooke Beauclere by the way,' she introduced herself, rectifying the omission.

'Adam Henderson.' He watched her carefully, but she made no response to the name, which was unfamiliar to her. Nor did he offer to shake her hand, instead, sliding his grip from her wrist to her hand, lifting it palm upwards to his mouth and placing his lips against it. The brush of his tongue against her palm made her jump in surprise, a thousand tiny nerve endings pulsing into life as his lips moved down to her fingers, nibbling erotically at her skin. When he finally released her hand she felt hot and disorientated. No one had ever made her feel like that before, but as she pulled herself together she reminded herself that practice makes perfect, and that no doubt he had learned long, long ago, just how to make a woman responsive to him. He certainly didn't look the type of man who would expect his partner to lie back and think of England, and he must want something for his money other than an unresponsively receptive body, Brooke thought cynically.

'Until tonight. . . .'

He let her go and watched her walk out of the door. Brooke was acutely conscious of his eyes on her back, and only realised when she got outside that she had been holding her breath.

A brisk walk down the drive to her lodge did much to restore her normal equilibrium, and by the time she reached the Lodge she was mentally berating herself for her stupidity. It must have been the wine, was her only excuse, but as she had drunk only the one glass it was a feeble one. Never one to deceive herself for long as she opened the door and braced herself to receive the enthusiastic embrace of her uncle's Afghan hound Brooke acknowledged that it was the man himself who had affected her, infuriating her to the point where she felt compelled to give the antagonism she had felt towards him an actual physical life.

'Down Balsebar,' she commanded the dog, grinning as he dropped pathetically to her feet. Balsebar was a dog of positive and slightly eccentric character; a true ham who loved playing to his audience. Right now he was doing a sterling impression of a down-trodden and mistreated innocent—a picture to tear at the heart of sweet old ladies and innocent children. Remembering his many escapades Brooke was unimpressed.

Black with golden paws and chest, his eyes could gleam with a wickedness that made him look almost devilish, but apart from his eccentric nature he was a first-rate guard dog. He also had an aversion to the male sex, excluding only her uncle, and Brooke grinned again at his possible reception of Adam Henderson. For some reason, despite all her determined efforts to stop him, Balsebar slept on the floor at the bottom of her bed—nothing could shift him from his chosen spot, and his normal reaction to any unwary male entering the Lodge was so craftily and cleverly worked out that the victim rarely knew what was happening to him until it was far too late. Not for Balsebar the reaction of other, less Machiavellian dogs—the frenzied barking or the doggy sulks. Every encounter involving Balsebar was a triumph of tactics and canine intelligence over his chosen human victim.

There had been the man who was allergic to dog hairs whose lap he had insisted on sitting on; there had been the one who had announced that he knew exactly the right way to handle recalcitrant dogs—no one was quite sure how it happened, but one moment he had been commanding Balsebar to 'sit', the next, for some reason the dog's claw had caught in the zip of his trousers as Balsebar leapt up in direct disobedience to his command and the poor man had been left standing in her uncle's drawing room with his trousers round his ankles and his rather stunning striped boxer undershorts on display to the world.

There had been countless others who had retreated in disorder, and Brooke wondered idly as she prepared his meal how Balsebar would deal with Adam Henderson. She also wondered how Adam would react when she told him she had changed her mind and that no matter how expensively he paid her she wouldn't go to bed with him. Now that she had left the party the tension which had led her to betraying her antagonism towards him had gone and in its stead was the uneasy knowledge that he was not a man who would take kindly to being duped. Her hand brushed the dog's head and he glanced up at her in mute enquiry. At least she could rely on Balsebar to defend her honour she thought wryly, even if she was incapable of doing so herself.

CHAPTER TWO

BY the time the grandfather clock in the small living room struck quarter to ten Brooke was an aching mass of too tense nerve endings, one moment mentally berating herself for her stupidity, the next telling herself that it was time that someone cut Adam Henderson down to size.

She had changed out of the suit she had worn to the cocktail party—an outfit left over from the days when she had worked as a secretary in an upmarket advertising agency and had had to dress accordingly. These days she thought herself fortunate if she was able to buy herself a decent skirt and blouse, never mind blowing half a month's salary on an expensive cocktail outfit. Glancing through her wardrobe she had dismissed most of its contents as unsuitable almost instantly—they were 'officey clothes', geared to executive lunches and board meetings. The odd dress she possessed was equally unsuitable, which left her normal uniform of jeans and a sweater or the pleated skirt and jumper she had worn when nursing Uncle James—he had hated the sight of women in trousers, and seemed to think that her soft heathery skirt and its toning cashmere jumpers were the right sort of thing for her to wear, and knowing how ill he really was she had purposely dressed to please him.

What did women normally wear in these circumstances? Her mind switched irresistibly to glamorous black silk négligés heavily trimmed

23

with lace; but somehow she couldn't imagine
Adam Henderson being impressed by such a
garment, even had she possessed one.

In the end she compromised with a plain black
skirt and a pretty cream angora jumper with some
self-embroidered detail on the boat-shaped neck-
line. She was still wearing the sheer silk stockings
she had worn beneath her suit and she left these
on, slipping her feet into a pair of lower heeled
shoes.

Ready by nine thirty, she had spent the
intervening fifteen minutes prowling restlessly
round the small living room, much to Balsebar's
annoyance.

Fifteen minutes later when the imperious rap on
the old-fashioned door knocker heralded Adam's
arrival, Balsebar did not, as other, less intelligent
canines were wont to do, burst into a volley of
barking. Instead he slid silently from his perch on
the chair he had adopted as his and padded
silently behind Brooke as she headed for the door.

The rooms in the Lodge were small, especially
when compared with both Abbot's Meade and the
Dower House that went with it, but that surely did
not account completely for the sense of suffocation
she experienced when Adam stepped into the tiny
hall, Brooke thought breathlessly.

Like her he had changed, switching the
formality of his dinner suit for a pair of dark
trousers in fine mohair and a white silk shirt, open
at the throat beneath a grey leather blouson jacket.

'Very prompt.' He congratulated her as she
closed the door behind her. Unlike his clothes his
manner was anything but casual, his grey eyes
moving over her with a gleam she recognised from
her days working at Harrods during the New Year

sale. Stepping hastily away she cannoned into Balsebar who signalled his disapproval with an unnerving howl.

Having seen the effect of this peculiarly nerve-shattering sound on the unsuspecting before, Brooke was a little surprised to see Adam's grin.

'Let that be a warning to you,' he murmured as he followed her into the sitting room, 'it isn't always wise to step too hard on a member of my sex.'

'Sometimes it's unavoidable,' Brooke snapped back feeling thoroughly unnerved, 'you will get underfoot.'

'What a strange attitude in a lovely lady. I thought that was where you loved having us—right under your dainty heels.'

'It appears to me that you have a very jaundiced view of the relationship between the sexes,' Brooke told him, indicating a bottle of sherry and asking if he would like a glass.

After briefly scrutinising the label he nodded his head. 'Full marks,' he told her accepting the glass she handed him. 'For some reason that escapes me, the majority of your sex seems to prefer a revoltingly sweet version of what is really a most pleasant drink. Perhaps they think it reinforces the sweetness inherent in their natures.'

'Or perhaps they think that your sex prefer pure syrup to something a little more astringent,' Brooke retaliated. A little to her surprise amusement tugged at the corners of his mouth. He was, she realised on a small start of shock, the most compellingly attractive man she had ever met, and not just on a physical level.

'Well,' he drawled in the soft way she was becoming familiar with, when he had finished his drink, 'that was the appetiser, now I'm ready for the main meal, but first. . . .'

Balsebar, who had thus far ignored the presence of their guest, got slowly to his feet as Adam produced his cheque book.

Watching him in fascinated horror Brooke saw him flick it open and produce a pen.

'You're very businesslike,' she managed to mutter faintly, hoping that the frail stem of her sherry glass wouldn't snap beneath the tense pressure of her fingers.

'I've found it pays.' Adam agreed urbanely. She wasn't quite in the same mould as his previous conquests, this tall redhead who was looking at him as though he had suddenly crawled out from under a stone. Fool, he mocked himself cynically, they're all the same inside the packaging, every last one of them, and this one had made no secret of the fact that she was available—at a price.

As though he sensed her tension Balsebar gave a warning growl deep in his throat, padding silently to Adam's side, the teeth that Brooke knew could deliver a painful little nip, slightly bared.

Adam merely laughed, and said, 'I think it might be best if we conduct the rest of our business upstairs—without the presence of your watchdog. As it is . . .' he glanced at his watch and frowned slightly, 'I have to be back by twelve, I'm expecting an overseas call. . . .'

His sheer cold-bloodedness made Brooke seethe. Even if she was madly, desperately in love with him, his attitude would chill her, freezing her into an inability to respond to him. Was he always like this, she wondered in awed fascination. If so, no wonder he had to pay his women to. . . . She shivered slightly her thoughts skidding to a standstill as she looked into his eyes. Cold he might seem outwardly, but inwardly. . . . The heat of that grey glance seemed to sear deep into her skin, warming her blood to a pulse beating rhythm that was totally alien and yet somehow intensely familiar.

'What's the matter? Having second thoughts?' The grey eyes narrowed; the effect of his total concentration on her almost hypnotic. It was very disturbing, this ability he seemed to have to follow her thoughts, and now perhaps was as good a time as any to let him see that on this occasion his male aggression and the power of his cheque book weren't going to be enough to get him what he wanted.

As this was the conclusion she had anticipated when she agreed to see him Brooke couldn't understand the too dry tension of her mouth; the emotion that could almost be fear which crawled down her spine. Unconsciously straightening her back she stared up at him. He must be at least six foot two she thought irrelevantly, because she had to tilt her head back to look him in the eyes—an advantage he was making full use of as he stared assessingly back at her.

'I'm afraid I am,' she agreed, giving him a small smile, 'Naughty of me isn't it?'

At any other time the sickening coyness of her response would have nauseated her, but now there was only a primaeval instinct for survival; an inner voice that urged her to turn and run and which she determinedly withstood, praying that the man standing opposite her wouldn't guess that her knees were shaking and that her stomach was churning sickeningly.

'Naughty?' One dark eyebrow rose. 'Oh I

wouldn't say that. Unwise perhaps . . . maybe even greedy. . . .' He moved as he spoke, grasping her arms with a swiftness that left her in a state of acute shock. No one had ever ignored the keep off signs she posted round her the way this man was doing.

The low growl coming from Balsebar's throat brought her back to reality, steadying her shaken nerves. 'I don't think Balsebar likes the way you're touching me,' she told Adam pleasantly. He looked at the dog, and to Brooke's disbelief he grinned.

Balsebar too seemed taken aback. He stopped growling and stared at him. Man and dog seemed to enter some silent male communication from which she was excluded, much to Brooke's frustration.

'Look, this has gone far enough,' she said tensely. 'Despite the outsize ego you possess which seems to lead you to believe you can simply walk in here and buy me, I'm really not interested in you—or your money.'

'No?' The slate eyes derided her. 'That wasn't how I heard it this afternoon.'

'That was this afternoon. This is tonight. . . .'

'Second thoughts? Or perhaps you simply want to be coaxed.' The cynical twist to his mouth made Brooke wonder how many other women he had put the question to.

'You want to believe there's more to it than merely sex, is that it? You're "not that kind of woman".' The savagery in his voice as he mimicked the words, sliced through her. 'I know all about the kind of woman you are,' he told her roughly, 'the kind who likes to play by the rules on the surface but who breaks them underneath it; the kind of woman who marries into the "right set" but who isn't above entertaining herself with someone from outside it, discreetly, of course. Oh yes, I know all about your kind of women—innate snobs who'd die rather than admit they can feel lust for a man of lower class; a man who doesn't play the game by their rules; who can't trace his ancestors back for half a dozen generations and who wasn't educated at the right schools. . . .'

'No. . . .' Brooke was genuinely horrified by his accusations. She knew exactly the sort of snobbery he referred to—she had seen it in action and to be given the label of the type of woman she most abhorred made her feel almost tainted.

'No? Then make good the promise you gave me,' he told her sardonically. One hand left her arm, his finger curling round her throat, his thumb lifting her chin, so that he could look into her eyes. 'Or do you want me to make it good for you, is that it?'

'All I want you to do is to leave here.' Brooke was more shaken than she wanted to admit. There was something about the rough abrasion of his hand against her skin that her body reacted to. It took an effort of will to drag her eyes from his face, and as she saw the shuttered contemptuous anger fill his eyes panic seized her. She struggled wildly to pull away from him, distantly conscious of Balsebar's warning bark, and the sudden flurry of black-and-gold fur as his teeth bit into the soft leather.

She heard Adam curse as he released her, staggering back under the weight of the dog. Never had she been more grateful for Balsebar's protection, she thought dizzily, mentally acknowledging that she had only herself to blame for her

present predicament. She should never have
allowed her own antagonism to reach the point
where she had felt compelled to strike a blow for
her own sex; the whole episode was rebounding
badly on her. Half expecting to hear Adam
demanding that she call off her guard dog, she was
stunned to see him reach round and prise the dog's
jaws out of his jacket. Balsebar was as surprised as
her, especially when lean fingers closed firmly
round his muzzle.

'I think the remainder of our discussion is best
conducted without this animal's interference.'
Adam told her grittily, and yet there was no
cruelty or anger in the way he grasped the dog's
collar or manoeuvred him into the kitchen, firmly
closing the door against any further intrusion.

'Now,' he said pleasantly, when he had
completed his task. His eyes weren't grey, they
were a devilish, dangerous black, Brooke thought
dismally, watching him advance towards her and
yet totally unable to do a single thing to evade
him.

'Where were we?'

'I was just telling you that I wanted you to
leave.'

'So you were, and I was just about to tell you
that I always get what I've paid for,' he told her
less pleasantly, indicating the cheque he had
placed on her coffee table. 'This . . .' he picked it
up and waved it tauntingly in front of her, 'entitles
me to certain. . . .'

Before he could continue Brooke wrenched the
cheque from his fingers and tore it to pieces,
flinging the scraps of paper on the fire.

'*Now* will you leave,' she demanded, knowing
that her cheeks were flushed with temper, and her

eyes glittering with the fear she could feel inching through her, driving out her normal composure.

'We made a bargain,' Adam reminded her softly, 'and I intend to make sure we both adhere to it.'

'You can't want me now, not knowing that I don't want you,' Brooke protested making a last desperate stand and measuring the distance between them. She was standing between Adam and the stairs; perhaps if she made a bolt for it, she could lock herself in the bathroom and sit it out until he decided to give up and leave. Undignified but . . . .

'Since I was never under that illusion in the first place, I don't see why. You sold yourself to me,' he reminded her. 'Or is that something else you've conveniently forgotton?'

It was the look in his eyes that did it, panicking her into a wild headlong flight up the stairs, which she knew that she had lost when she heard him behind her. He grabbed her just as she reached the landing, his breathing still under control where hers was rapid and erratic. By some misfortune he had caught her just outside her bedroom door—it stood open, the old-fashioned half tester bed plainly in view.

'Well, well, how convenient,' he drawled, following her dismayed glance.'

Despite her height he picked her up as though she were a doll, kicking the door closed with one foot, and advancing towards the bed.

Having expected to be flung down on it, it came as a surprise to Brooke to find herself standing upright, Adam's fingers manacling her wrists.

'Well now,' he drawled softly, 'there are two ways of doing this. You can admit defeat—

gracefully and charmingly as befits a lady . . .' his voice lingered insolently over the noun, 'or we can indulge in a little of the rough and tumble it seems so many of you *ladies* enjoy—a relic of the days when that was the way your ancestors won their rich brides perhaps? Which is it to be?'

He looked so controlled and indifferent, standing there watching her, that Brooke could hardly believe what she was hearing.

'Either way it will be rape,' she told him coldly. Too late now to bitterly regret her foolhardiness. Who was this man anyway? Her blood chilled as she remembered news stories of women abused and then murdered. Was this man. . . .

The sound of his laughter as it filled the room, warm and genuine, threw her, stopping her terror-stricken thoughts in their tracks.

'A nice try my dear, but hardly applicable.' One hand unclasped her wrist, his thumb running slightly and tormentingly over the soft fullness of her bottom lip.

'You have the most sensuously inviting mouth I've ever seen, and I wanted to feel it beneath mine, sweet and hot, the moment I set eyes on you. You're no young girl just out of school to plead innocence and ignorance. You know exactly what you do to me when you look at me with those green-gold eyes.'

'Rape . . . ' he laughed again. 'It might be worth calling your bluff.'

He said it so with so much calm self-assurance that something inside Brooke snapped. Like all the others he couldn't see beyond her looks; didn't *want* to see beyond them. Just for a moment she wanted to hurt him as painfully as he had just hurt her.

'Well, Brooke, which is it to be?' His voice was soft, mesmeric almost, his thumb probing the closed line of her lips, its roughness oddly pleasant against her smooth skin. His other hand was travelling up her arm, his thumb tracing the line of the blue vein that pulsed against her skin. Anger and despair mingled in an explosive reaction. Brooke opened her mouth, her teeth snapping defensively against his thumb. Just in time he realised what she intended to do and drew back.

This time when his eyes darkened she was in no doubts about the emotions she saw mirrored there. Anger and a desire so intense that it stunned her. This time she was flat on her back, fighting for breath and for freedom as the weight of his body kept her there, precious little finesse in his actions as her angora jumper was pushed up to reveal the soft thrust of her breasts in her cream silk bra. The delicate cups were pushed aside as cavalierly as her jumper had been.

'Very well, if this is the way you want it'

She opened her mouth to protest and then closed it quickly sucking air into her deprived lungs, torn between humiliated shock and a tearing, searing pleasure that invaded her body when Adam opened his mouth over the centre of one rounded breast and tugged impatiently at the soft pink crest.

Her body's response was electrically immediate. No one had ever touched her so intimately, and intermingled with a bitter fury that he should dare to do so was an undeniable physical response. Her body had gone rigid with the shock of his intimacy, her mind spiralling wildly out of her control as she fought to marshall her defences, but before she could utter a word Adam was releasing her, pulling her into a sitting position and matter-of-factly straightening her clothes, the sudden about-face stunning her.

'Well, well,' he drawled when he had finished. 'You *are* a surprise package, aren't you?'

'Am I?' Brooke's chin tilted belligerently. Now that Adam was no longer touching her a little of her courage filtered back.

'Well, there can't be many virgins of your age still left,' he told her mockingly. 'You must be in your mid-twenties, and when one takes into consideration all your many physical attri-butes. . . .' His glance slid insolently over her body, resting for several seconds on the soft curve of her breasts. Remembering how he had caressed them only minutes before Brooke felt her face go a deep and unhideable scarlet.

'You're not gay are you?'

The matter-of-fact question stunned her into fresh silence, and then he started to laugh again, further adding to her humiliation. 'No, something tells me that you're not, so that doesn't leave us with many alternatives does it? Are you going to tell me why, or are we going to sit here all night playing guessing games until I find out,' he asked her pleasantly.

This can't really be happening, was Brooke's first thought. She had expected him to be furiously angry when she rejected him, which he had been, but this unexpected turn of events totally flummoxed her.

'Why should you want to know?' She was dismayed to hear herself sounding like a sulky, petulant adolescent.

'Oh for a variety of reasons, including the very natural curiosity of any man who a woman chooses as her first lover.'

Once she had assimilated the implications of his remark Brooke flushed angrily again.

'I did not *choose* you as my lover,' she stormed back at him. 'You made totally false suppositions about me which led you to believe that I was sexually available—at a price,' she finished bitterly.

'And you did nothing to deny those suppositions,' he reminded her calmly, adding, 'and something tells me that I'm far from being the first male to make them. Is that the reason you're still a virgin?'

He was far too astute Brooke recognised on a wave of trepidation. Far, far too astute.

'You can hardly blame them you know,' he added grinning at her. 'That mouth . . .' he traced the outline of it with his thumb before she could retreat out of range, 'in fact everything about you, possesses an earthy sensuality that can't help but turn men on.'

'Looks, is that all your sex concern themselves with?' Brooke derided angrily, 'Don't bother to answer,' she told him. 'I already know the answer. . . .'

'And because of that you're waiting for Prince Charming to turn up? The perfect lover who you will fall blissfully in love with and live with happily ever after?'

'I don't believe in love—at least not that variety,' Brooke told him coldly. 'Friendship is more important to a relationship than sexual desire—it lasts longer too. My parents were friends first and lovers second.'

'How very cynical,' Adam derided gently.

'No, just practical,' was Brooke's heated

response. 'You see I've seen what happens to women when they believe they've fallen in love and I don't want that for me. If I ever marry I want a husband who respects me as a person, someone who'll never treat me as a second-class citizen, a physical convenience who he'll tire of and want to discard the moment I'm no longer young and attractive enough to swell his ego. I'd like you to go now,' she added lamely, knowing that she had told him more about herself in ten short minutes than she had told other people in almost a life time. 'I'm sorry about ... about leading you on. . . .'

'Mmm ... why did you?'

'I didn't like your attitude,' Brooke told him honestly. 'I resented your assumption that I was available to you provided you were willing to pay. When I share the act of love with a man it will be because it is something that we both want; not merely because either of us wants to satisfy a brief sexual need.'

She felt him tense as he studied her through narrowed silver-grey eyes that carefully blanked off whatever he might be feeling.

'Well, Brooke Beauclere, tonight I think we've both learned something we didn't know before, don't you?' He leaned forward, smiling with faint malice as she edged away from him. 'No need to look at me like that, virgins, no matter how appealing, aren't quite my line, but just to add to your education and to reward myself for my forbearance.' His mouth brushed hers, the brief contact electrifying. She had been kissed before, many times, but never like this Brooke acknowledged meltingly as his mouth continued to explore and tease hers, firm, masculine lips tracing the tremulous outlines of the mouth she was unable to keep still.

When the roughly persuasive stroke of his tongue was added to the sensual torment, something seemed to unfurl inside her. White teeth nipped erotically at the full lower curve of her mouth, Adam's tongue making full use of the advantage her silent gasp gave him to invade beyond the barrier of her teeth.

Sensations so unexpectedly pleasurable that they stunned her jammed all the warning signals of her brain, her hands going instinctively to Adam's shoulders, her body barely registering the fact that he was pushing her back against her bed, or that his hand was caressing the full warmth of her breast, his thumb and finger teasing the burgeoning hardness of her nipple.

Heat seemed to envelop her body; a heat so intense and unexpected that she trembled with the force of it. When Adam released her, for several seconds she could do no more than stare blankly up at him, unable to understand how he could have conjured up a response from the body that had hitherto obeyed her every command.

'I like that,' he told her softly, still smiling. 'I like knowing that I can make you respond to me, and that no man has ever touched you or kissed you the way I was just doing. They haven't, have they Brooke?'

She wanted to deny his arrogantly self-assured claim; to tell him that just because she was a virgin it didn't mean she had no sexual experience at all, but caution intervened. Adam had more than enough experience to know when she was lying; her almost adolescent reaction to him was hardly that of an experienced woman; and she doubted that he would be very impressed by the inept fumblings of her early teenage years, dismissing them with the same mocking contempt that he would use to decimate her lies, if she was foolish enough to speak them.

'No,' she admitted reluctantly, 'but it won't happen again, Adam. I don't want to see you again. . . .'

'You haven't been asked,' he reminded her tauntingly, adding. 'I can let myself out. Sleep well won't you?'

He had been gone for over ten minutes before Brooke could rouse herself sufficiently to go down and let Balsebar out of the kitchen. The dog was patently aggrieved, almost as though it was her fault he had been incarcerated there in the first place. Which in a way it was Brooke admitted, opening the back door to let him out. In the cool darkness of the autumn evening her skin heated betrayingly—thank goodness she was never likely to see Adam Henderson again she reflected, as Balsebar emerged from the garden and followed her inside. She wouldn't let herself think about what might have happened if he hadn't recognised her virginal inexperience. His mood hadn't been kind when he had manhandled her into the bedroom and she shivered, recognising that he could be a very dangerous enemy if he chose to be. But not *her* enemy; not anything in *her* life except an error of judgment she had made which had had potentially embarrassing repercussions. Know your own limitations my girl, she chided herself as she locked the back door . . . don't jump into deep water like that again. Now it was difficult to conjure up the feeling of antagonism that had urged her to confront him in the first place; in fact the entire episode, from meeting him to his leavetaking tonight, already seemed to be part of a dream; totally unreal and inappropriate to her normal everyday life.

Forget him, she urged herself as she prepared for bed. Forget him, and concentrate on how you're going to support yourself from now on.

The Lodge was hers outright and she had a bank balance of some few thousand pounds. That her solicitor thought she was mad to donate what was left of the purchase money from Abbot's Meade to the local children's hospital she knew quite well, but they were doing research there on all forms of children's cancer and from the conversations with her uncle's doctor Brooke knew how badly they needed extra funds. She could get herself a job; she was old enough and intelligent enough to support herself, unlike those poor children. A job ... she sighed ... she would have to start looking round, although she suspected that Sam was right when he said that a secretary of her calibre was hardly likely to find a suitable position locally.

Not even to herself was she prepared to admit that she might be using her mental busyness concerning her lack of employment to cover deeper and even more disturbing thoughts. That Adam Henderson had affected her as no man had ever done before, she could not deny, but she certainly wasn't prepared to admit that there was anything especially significant in the fact that he had done so; it had simply been a question of fate running with him and against her, and she doubted that he was ever likely to have exactly that dynamic effect on her ever again.

CHAPTER THREE

'COME on now, Uncle Sam, give. You were very mysterious on the telephone this morning. What's all this about you finding a job for me?'

They were sitting in Sam Brockbank's office in the small market town of Abbot's Meade. The office was as familiar to Brooke as the rooms of Abbot's Meade itself, and she surveyed the untidy clutter with a rueful smile as she watched her solicitor shuffle the untidy piles of paper on his desk.

'Well it isn't so much that I've found you a job,' he told her cautiously, 'it's more that I've been approached to tell you that one exists, if you are interested.'

'Mysteriouser and mysteriouser,' Brooke quipped lightly, 'Don't keep me in suspense. Tell me all about it.'

She had dressed for her meeting in one of the neat suits she had worn during her London days—a soft melding of pink and blue tweeds that should have clashed horribly with her hair but did not, her cream silk blouse a perfect foil for her pale skin.

'The chairman of Hart Enterprises is looking for a PA, and apparently he's prepared to offer you the job.'

'Just like that?' Brooke raised her eyebrows. She had heard of Hart Enterprises first when she worked for the advertising agency and its chairman had the reputation of being particularly

40

ruthless. Hart Enterprises never carried dead or excessive wood, and she could think of no single reason why she should be invited to join the staff. She was a good secretary, with first rate qualifications and excellent speeds and she knew that her last boss had been sorry to lose her, but surely Hart Enterprises already employed a dozen or more girls equally as skilled as she was herself. Unless of course the chairman was the sort of ogre who demolished secretaries for breakfast.

She watched Sam clear his throat, avoiding her eyes as he re-shuffled his papers. Apparently he's heard about you in the City . . . and when I mentioned that you were looking for a job. . . .'

'He jumped at the opportunity to take me on to his staff?' Brooke supplied drily. It wasn't impossible that he might indeed have heard of her; the agency did a considerable amount of work for Hart Enterprises, but she suspected that Sam was the one who was responsible for the unexpected job offer. 'It's very good of you Sam,' she told him, softening her firmness with a slight smile, 'but I don't intend to rely on the "old boy network" to get myself a job. . . .'

'Nothing of the kind,' her solicitor was quick to assure her. 'He genuinely does want an assistant, Brooke. Although Abbot's Meade will need to have a great deal of work done on it before it's ready to operate as the Corporation's headquarters, the chairman plans to move into the Dower House almost immediately and supervise both the work and his business interests from there. That's why he was so keen to interview you. Apparently his present secretary is expecting a baby and on the point of leaving.'

'Well, I don't suppose it would do any harm to

attend the interview,' Brooke agreed, knowing that she was weakening, but the job sounded far too promising for her to dismiss out of hand. From the little her solicitor had told her about it, it sounded just the sort of challenge she was in need of right now to take her mind off losing Abbot's Meade, and . . . other things.

'If you're interested, an interview's been arranged for this afternoon.'

'Short notice isn't it?'

'Apparently the chairman's pretty anxious to get things moving. He doesn't like hanging around, waiting for things; wasting time. . . .'

'So I've heard,' Brooke agreed dryly, searching her memory for any scraps of information stored there regarding her potential employers. Hart Enterprises' reputation was a first-rate one; their work highly acclaimed; one of their specialities was the renovation of old houses such as Abbot's Meade, and indeed that had been one of the factors that had encouraged her to sell to Hart Enterprises in the first place. The job did sound tempting, but she wasn't too sure if she was happy with the fact that Uncle Sam had apparently pushed her forward as a candidate for it. Telling herself that she had nothing to lose in attending the interview she bid him goodbye, and emerged from the gloomy clutter of his office into the bright November sunshine.

The autumn had been a dry one, and the rich colours of autumn leaves gathered in drifts in the gutters. Repressing a childish temptation to swish through them, Brooke headed through the small town square to the municipal car park where she had left her bike.

As always her progress was impeded by several

people wanting to chat to her about the sale of the house and its possible implications for the town.

'Should bring in a sight more business,' one matron told Brooke, 'they say they're going to turn the stables into flats for them as works up at the house?'

Gently parrying the question Brooke hurried on her way. She had heard that Hart's intended to convert the old stable block into mews apartments and the drawings she had been shown had depicted a very attractive conversion, with the old stable yard still retaining its cobbles but decorated with tubs of flowers and turned into a communal garden.

It was lunchtime before she got back to the Lodge, her progress delayed by the swift passage of a black Ferrari, taking up more than its fair share of the drive. It was being driven too fast for her to see the driver, and as she was forced to wait before turning into the drive Brooke reflected that such inconveniences were something she was going to have to get used to.

After eating a light lunch she took Balsebar out for his walk. In the past she had always let him run loose in the park, but now she decided against this—after all the grounds were no longer hers, and instead clipped on his lead and took him over the stile into the fields beyond which had once belonged to Abbot's Meade, as part of the home farm but which had long ago been sold off.

A bare, golden stubble decorated the fields, birds scratching amongst it for food. The hedgerows shone scarlet with berries and as she drew in lungfuls of clean, fresh air, Brooke decided that she was not sorry not to be returning to London.

Back at the Lodge she brushed her hair, and re-applied her make-up, changing out of the jeans and sweater she had worn to walk Balsebar, back into her tweed suit.

Although she normally enjoyed the walk from the Lodge to the house, on this occasion she felt very tense. If the chairman of Hart Enterprises was as formidable as his reputation suggested she didn't want to arrive wind-blown and hot. As she walked up to the house Bill Edwards watched her from an upstairs window, sighing faintly and glancing at his watch. When Adam had told him what he had arranged he had been dumbfounded. Adam's affairs were legion; common knowledge among his senior staff, but this was the first time in all the years that Bill had known him that he had ever contemplated mixing business with pleasure.

Whatever her other attributes might or might not be Brooke Beauclere was certainly a very, very attractive woman, Bill thought appreciatively watching the elegant swing of her body as she walked towards the building. She carried her height well, and her stride was that of a woman who feels confident and at home with her body. Oh yes, he could well understand why Adam was so keen to pursue the chase, but Adam was notorious for his cold detached view of everything he did. Once he had captured his prey he would no longer be interested in her—that was what always happened—but if the woman was employed by Hart Enterprises?

Sighing Bill turned his attention back to studying the résumé which had arrived by special messenger only half an hour ago. Reading it he couldn't help but be impressed by Brooke's qualifications. She appeared to have all the attributes necessary to make a first rate PA, but he doubted, after seeing that flaming banner of red hair, that she could match Adam's clinical detachment once their affair was over.

Having knocked on the door and been told to enter, Brooke was slightly surprised to be confronted by a mild-looking man in his early thirties, who responded to her evident surprise with a slight smile.

'Bill Edwards,' he introduced himself, 'I'm sorry that out chairman can't interview you himself. He's been called away on urgent business, but I am empowered to offer you the job, provided we can both agree that you and it are well matched. Please sit down.'

The interview was a pleasant one. He asked Brooke a little about the history of the house, which she willingly told him.

'There's always a sense of sadness at the passing of these old families,' he sympathised when she had explained that her uncle had been the last male Meade, 'although presumably if you had a son the title could be revived?'

'I should think so, but it's hardly important,' Brooke told him. 'I believe Mr Hart intends to occupy the Dower House himself?'

Noting the 'Mr Hart' Bill frowned slightly. He had been pretty sure that during the cocktail party Adam had made arrangements to see the girl again. She didn't look like the type well-schooled in deception and the 'Mr Hart' had tripped naturally off her tongue. Neither, now that he had a closer look at her, did she resemble Adam's normal conquests. Her chin was too determined somehow, and she met his look quite frankly and openly. 'How do you think you will like working for Mr Hart?' he questioned her thoughtfully, watching her reaction.

'I'm not really sure—not having met him, but if he's prepared to take me on as his PA sight unseen, then. . . .'

Suppressing a sigh Bill wondered if he ought to tell her that she most certainly had met 'Mr Hart', and then decided against it. Coward, he taunted himself, as he wound up the interview, but Adam had left him with specific instructions. He wanted Brooke Beauclere as his PA.

When he mentioned Brooke's salary, naming the same sum as Adam's present PA earned Brooke raised her eyebrows and looked rather stunned. 'That's very generous, isn't it?' she queried.

'It's exactly what Betty—Mr Hart's present PA earns.'

'But surely that's with a London weighting allowance. . . .'

Bill laughed. 'You're the first prospective employee I've ever interviewed who's tried to negotiate her salary downwards.' He found himself liking her more and more, *and* worrying more and more about her ability to cope with Adam, but felt honour-bound not to say anything to her. Adam *was* his boss and a good one, he owed him his loyalty and his livelihood.

'There's just one thing,' he said as he stood up to escort Brooke to the door. 'Mr Hart would like you to start here on Monday morning. It's extremely convenient having you living at the Lodge. He'll be moving into the Dower House over the weekend and initially you'll be working from there. . . .'

'But the place is practically derelict,' Brooke

told him. 'It's been empty since our last tenants left and that's three years ago.'

'We're moving in a team to check it over today. Just as long as A . . . Mr Hart can have a terminal set up linked to our main computer he can work, although I believe he intends to supervise the renovations here himself. You don't think you'll find that too painful?' He was making a last ditch attempt to dissuade her from taking the job, without being seen to do so, Bill acknowledged, but Brooke shook her head. 'Sentiment of that kind is something I can't afford right now,' she told him simply, extending her hand to shake his. On her feet, she was an inch or so taller than he was himself, Bill thought ruefully, beautifully composed, and coolly remote; the thought of what Adam could and probably would do to that fragile shell of hauteur made him cringe in anticipation of her pain, but there was nothing he could do about it, and for the first time since he had come to work for Adam, he found himself almost actively disliking him.

'Monday morning then at the Dower House,' Brooke said with a smile. 'I'm already looking forward to it; the job sounds extremely challenging.'

Far more challenging than she could yet imagine, Bill thought worriedly, but there was nothing he could do to warn her.

She had been gone half an hour when his 'phone rang and he picked it up, already anticipating who his caller would be.

'Did she accept the job?'

Adam had never been one to waste words uselessly.

'Yes,' Bill was equally terse, 'although she thought the salary was too high.'

A little to his surprise Adam laughed. 'That's my girl,' he drawled lightly. 'And did you manage to restrain yourself from warning her that she's about to step into the big bad wolf's lair?'

Adam saw and knew far too much Bill thought a little bitterly. 'Yes, but I don't like myself for doing it.'

Saturday was as bright and sunny as the weathermen had promised, and Brooke decided to make good use of the bright spell to tidy up the Lodge garden. She was midway through brushing up dead leaves and building a bonfire when the black Ferrari swept through the open gates, followed by a small van.

So the Ferrari must belong to her new boss, she reflected thoughtfully watching them disappear. Strange, she had for some reason had him pegged as a chauffeur-driven Rolls man. Returning to her task she dismissed him from her mind. Time enough to worry about her new job on Monday morning. Right now she needed the breathing space of this weekend. Tonight she was having dinner with Sam, his wife and their daughter and son-in-law, and if she knew Mary, she would have found a 'spare man' from somewhere to partner her. A small smile tugged at the corners of her mouth. She liked Mary very much, but knew that the older woman thought it was high time that she found herself a husband. Mary was a perennial romantic who believed in falling in love and living happily ever after. She repressed a slight smile as she envisaged Mary's views on the fact that the only man to arouse any feelings at all in her was quite definitely not likely to fall head over heels in love with her, and furthermore had anything but marriage on his mind!

Stop thinking about him, she warned herself as she finished gathering up the leaves. It was a once and for all encounter and be grateful for that fact, otherwise the chances are that. . . .

That what? That she would end up in his bed? Never, she told herself firmly. Okay; she had been physically attracted to him, but physical attraction didn't stop her brain from working and her brain told her loudly and clearly that he was strictly a man who liked playing games; a no commitment, no comebacks man who she doubted ever even considered looking more than skin deep at the woman he was with. Definitely not her type at all; and her momentary response to him had been nothing more than an unfortunate mistake.

It was late afternoon before she had finished tidying up the garden. There had been a certain physical satisfaction to be found in digging and weeding and now her body ached pleasantly, the scent of her bonfire lingering in the still early evening air.

She called Balsebar as she trudged towards the Lodge with her tools, sighing faintly when the dog didn't materialise. No doubt he had escaped into the park; like her he seemed to be having difficulty in accepting that it was now out of bounds to him. A sharp whistle brought him back, and as they went inside he nudged Brooke affectionately with his long nose. She was still a little surprised at how easily Adam had handled him the previous night.

There had been gentleness as well as firmness in the way he had controlled the dog, restraining him without trying to master him. Would he handle a woman with the same firm confidence? Somehow the question slipped past her guard and into her mind, to be instantly banished.

Stop thinking about him, she abjured herself as she went upstairs to run a bath and prepare for the evening ahead.

She was just putting the finishing touches to her make-up when the 'phone rang. The absurd sense of disappointment she felt when she recognised Mary's voice challenged all her brave mental assurances that Adam Henderson had made no real emotional impression on her.

'Just to tell you that you needn't cycle tonight dear,' Mary explained. 'Jeff Gibson will be picking you up. Remember him?'

Jeff Gibson had originally been one of Sam's articled clerks, but it was several years since he had left the district. Brooke did remember him though, as a rather spotty, shy individual who had lurked in a corner of the outer office every time she went into the solicitor's.

'Vaguely,' she agreed, hiding a small smile. Mary was matchmaking again.

She was ready on the dot of eight; her plain black velvet dress swirling softly round her legs as she hurried to answer the doorbell, at the same time restraining Balsebar.

Her initial thought was that the spots had gone and that in the intervening years Jeff had obviously filled out and lost his diffidence. Balsebar expressed low-growled disapproval as he followed Brooke into the hall.

'I'll just get my coat,' she told him, shooing the dog away. 'I won't be a second.' As she hurried upstairs she was conscious of Jeff admiring the long length of her legs and suddenly the evening which she had suspected might be rather dreary took on a new aspect.

The hair she remembered as cut very short and slightly mousy was now much longer and the same sun that had given his skin its deep tan had bleached the ends. In all Jeff Gibson was a very attractive man, and she liked the way he helped her into the car, taking care not to touch her in any way that wasn't strictly conventional—unlike some of her escorts.

It was only a short drive to Sam's. Jeff chatted about old acquaintances as he drove, explaining that he had been working in America and that he had come back to deal with his mother's small estate.

Brooke had only a dim memory of his mother who she remembered had lived in the town, but she expressed her sympathy when Jeff told her that she had died several weeks previously.

'I wasn't looking forward to tonight,' he told her frankly as they turned into the road leading to the Brockbanks. 'My last memory of you is with pigtails and freckles.'

'Mine of you is equally flattering,' Brooke told him with a smile.

'Umm, I can imagine.' The sideways glance he gave her was extremly amused. 'I refused to believe it when Mary told me you'd turned into a raving beauty, but I can see that she was quite right.' He glanced at her bare ring finger. 'No attachments?'

'No. And you?' It was one of her rules never to date, no matter how casually, attached males.

'I was married, but that's over now I'm divorced. Until my mother died I was firmly convinced that my future lay in the States. I've built up a good practice there, but since I've been back here I'm not so sure. . . . There's something about the place where your roots lie.'

'Yes, I know,' Brooke agreed.

The subject was dropped as they stopped at their destination, but after the flurry of greetings was over and they were all sitting round Mary's attractively decorated dinner table, it was re-surrected again.

'I'm trying to persuade Jeff here to come into partnership with me,' Sam told her. 'Mary's keen for me to retire.'

'And I must say I'm very tempted,' Jeff told him. 'Even more so after tonight,' he added with a grin and an appreciative look at Brooke.

Brooke knew and liked Sam's daughter and her husband, and the evening was an exceptionally convivial one. So much so that she was almost disappointed when Jeff suggested it was time for them to go.

'It's gone twelve,' he told her with a charmingly apologetic smile, 'and I'm afraid I have to be in London quite early tomorrow. I promised to meet a friend who's flying in from Dallas on the early morning flight.'

They drove back to the Lodge in a companion-able silence and when Jeff drew up outside it and stopped Brooke turned to him and said with a smile, 'I won't invite you in for coffee in view of your early start in the morning, but it's been a most enjoyable evening. . . .'

'Indeed it has, and this adds the perfect finishing touch,' he murmured, bending his head to kiss her.

His mouth was mobile and experienced and although the sensation of it moving against her own was not distasteful, there was none of the explosive response she had experienced with Adam

Henderson. Jeff made no attempt to stop her when she pulled away from him, simply bending his head to kiss her lightly once more.

As he did so, car headlights flashed into the interior of his parked car, the long low shape of a black Ferrari snarling past them and on up the drive.

'Who was that?' Jeff asked, obviously startled by the interruption.

'My new boss,' Brooke told him flippantly, quickly explaining the situation to him, as she reached for the car door and opened it. 'It's been a lovely evening, Jeff.'

'The first of many I hope,' he said softly, coming round to help her out of the car before reversing and driving away.

On Sunday morning Brooke was up early, reading her newspapers over a mug of coffee when she heard Balsebar's warning bark. Frowning slightly she put down the paper and glanced through the window. She wasn't expecting anyone. . . . Her heart started to thump in unexpected recognition as she saw Adam Henderson walking towards her front door. For one cowardly moment she toyed with the idea of pretending she wasn't in, only to dismiss the thought as childishly irrational.

As she opened the door to him she wondered where he'd come from. Somehow she had thought he must by now have returned to London along with the majority of the other guests at the cocktail party. A little to her surprise, Balsebar, who had followed her to the door, greeted him quite warmly, fanning his whip thin tail against the floor.

'Hello boy.' Lean fingers stroked the black coat

and Brooke was appalled by the sensations the sight of them stirred through her blood, her brusquely defensive, 'What do you want?' causing black eyebrows to climb steeply, a slight smile curving the corners of his mobile mouth.

'Well that's a fine way to treat your new neighbour I must say.' Adam taunted. 'The least I expected was an offer of a mug of that delicious-smelling coffee and a cup of sugar.'

Neighbour? Brooke stared at him in consternation. 'What do you mean?'

'Come on Brooke,' the soft voice taunted, 'according to that very impressive recommendation your previous employers gave us you're an exceptionally intelligent and keen-witted girl. What do you think it means?'

He was looking at her in a way she didn't much like, amusement fanning tiny lines round his eyes, his expression almost smug.

'I'm not quite sure.' She was stalling for time. 'The nearest house to mine is the Dower House.'

'Full marks so far. . . .'

'But that's occupied by the chairman of Hart Enterprises,' she continued slowly. What was it about this man that warned her not to trust him a single inch.

'Your new boss,' Adam agreed, showing his teeth in an openly wolfish smile.

'You're staying with him?' Brooke hazarded, sensing that he was about to spring a carefully baited trap, watching him warily.

'Him?'

'Mr Hart.'

'Ah . . . that would be Mr Adam Henderson Hart?'

He didn't need to say any more. Brooke's face

paled and for a second she was tempted to slam the door in his face. Anticipating her his foot was already wedged inside it, the solid muscularity of his shoulder forcing it open.

'You tricked me,' she accused angrily. 'You knew I would never agree to work for you. And I won't. . . .'

'Why not?' He was smiling at her with lazy appreciation, watching the flurried rise and fall of her breasts beneath the thin wool of her jumper. Just having him standing there made her nerves tense up like too finely tuned violin strings. Something about him made her feel edgy and jumpy as a nervous cat.

'I can't work with you after. . . .'

'After what happened the other night? Why not? Frightened that next time you might not be able to fend me off so easily, nor want to?' His voice dropped over the last few words and Brooke was unable to prevent the rich tide of colour flooding over her skin.

'No ... because I can't work at optimum capacity if I'm constantly having to field sexist remarks like that,' she told him heatedly. 'I can't understand why you want me working for you anyway. . . .'

'Can't you?' There was definite amusement in the grey eyes as they lifted to search her angry, tense face. 'And you're positive that you prefer flight to fight? What is it you're so frightened of Brooke?'

'I'm not frightened,' she denied hastily, sensing that not to do so would be to give him an irrefutable advantage.

'No? Then prove it,' he mocked softly. 'Come and work for me and prove to me that you're as indifferent to me as I know you're longing to tell me you are.'

He had read her mind with devastating accuracy. She was caught in a trap, Brooke recognised. If she refused to work for him now she sensed that it would not end there. He wanted her and he was prepared to pursue her mercilessly. Her only means of defence was to face him; to stand up to him and prove to him that her defences were impenetrable.

'Very well.' Her chin jutted obstinately. 'But on the strict understanding that our relationship is purely a business one.'

'If that's the way you want it. How about sealing the bargain with a cup of coffee?' he suggested. 'I'm dying for a cup.'

Somehow or other Brooke found herself on her way back to her kitchen with Adam and Balsebar on her heels. When she had poured him his coffee and they were both sitting down he looked and said softly, 'Well, did you enjoy it when he kissed you?'

She was so startled that she nearly spilled her drink, and then she remembered the black Ferrari. She had thought at the time that it was an unusual choice of car for the chairman of Hart Enterprises, but then she had not known the identity of the chairman. He had deliberately deceived her. She looked up at him and he said impassively, 'Answer my question first, and then I'll answer yours.'

Chin jutting Brooke said truculently, 'Yes, I did—very much. . . .'

'But not enough to let him take you to bed,' Adam came back softly. 'Not as much as you enjoyed my kisses.'

Hot colour seeped up under her skin caused not

this time by embarrassment but by anger. 'That's not true,' she began heatedly, but the words were crushed against her mouth as Adam stood up with one easy powerful movement and hauled her into his arms, his mouth punishing hers for its lies, his tongue probing and stroking until she was enmeshed in a reason-destroying web of molten pleasure.

'We made a bargain.' Brooke choked fiercely when he eventually released her.

'But you're not officially working for me yet,' Adam reminded her. 'Now tell me again that you don't like my kisses.'

The words burned in her throat but Brooke knew she would not utter them. Her lips felt soft and vulnerable, acutely sensitive to the rough pressure of Adam's against them; in fact her whole body was acutely aware of him in a way she had never imagined being aware of any man. She could smell the faint odour of his cologne, tangy and masculine and beneath it the scent of fresh clean skin. She could remember quite vividly the rough rasp of his jaw against her face; the power of his fingers biting into her arms.

'Why did you lie to me about your name?' she managed thickly, her tongue unruly as she tried to get it round the accusing words.

'I didn't lie, I simply avoided giving you all of it. You said yourself you were up for sale,' he reminded her lazily. 'My name has a way of upping the price—that's the only reason; there was no ulterior motive.'

'Why do you want me to work for you?'

He laughed, a soft sound deep in his throat. 'Why *don't* you want to?' he mocked. 'It's an excellent job; interesting, well paid, with a variety of fringe benefits.' Something in the way he said the last few words made Brooke look closely at him, but there was nothing to be read from his impassive features. 'Be there tomorrow morning Brooke,' he warned her as he stood away from her and reached for the door. 'Be there!'

CHAPTER FOUR

'AND this is going to be my study.' Adam stepped to one side to allow Brooke to precede him into what had been the Dower House Library. The shelves she remembered as muddled and filled with mildewed books had been cleared and cleaned; a large desk complete with sophisticated technical computer equipment dominated the room.

'Know anything about these?' Adam glanced from Brooke to the computer terminal.

'A little,' she responded cautiously. 'I did a short course of computer technology when I was with Barrards, but this looks far more sophisticated than the terminal I used.'

'If you know the basics you'll soon pick it up,' Adam told her casually. 'There'll be a full-sized computer room at Abbot's Meade eventually, but right now I'm having to make do with this. It's linked to the main computer at our Head Office in London, and it means that I can keep in touch with what's going on but remain here to check on progress with the conversion of the house.'

'If you already have a head office in London I can't see why you bought Abbot's Meade?' Brooke had dressed with special care for this her first morning as Adam's PA. When she arrived half an hour ago she had addressed him as 'Mr Hart' but he had soon disabused her of the idea that he intended to allow her to put such a formal gulf between them. 'Call me "Adam",' he told her curtly, 'My last PA did.'

'Partially with the future in mind and partially as a showpiece. Hart's are becoming more and more involved with restoration work on old buildings—we have built up good contacts with various craftsmen and we're beginning to get a name for this type of work. Abbot's Meade, once restored, as I intend it to be restored will provide a show place for those crafts—it will give some of our more cautious clients a physical example of what can be done.'

'Especially when they see the computer room,' Brooke said dryly. 'Where's that going to go? In the Georgian Library?'

She was surprised to see a dark edge of colour creeping angrily up under Adam's tan. 'I'm not quite the philistine you seem to believe,' he told her tersely. 'All right I don't have Bill's public school education; and my family certainly wasn't out of the "top drawer" but that doesn't mean I can't appreciate the workmanship and value of what Abbot's Meade offers, and unlike your ancestors *I* at least have the wealth to preserve it.'

His angry words took Brooke aback. She had merely been teasing him a little and had not expected such a bitterly violent reaction, 'As it happens the computer room will be housed in one of the cellars—the main rooms of the house will be restored to their original state—or as close to it as possible, and will be used when we entertain overseas guests and for small conferences.' He frowned and walked over to his desk. 'There's a book here I found on these shelves when they were being cleared out. It's some sort of diary and mentions the decor in the Dower House as it must have been when it was built.'

'Yes, that's right,' Brooke agreed following him

over to the desk and glancing at the book he indicated. 'The Dower House was designed and decorated by Adam—and apparently was something of rarity when it was first built.'

'I was wondering if there was anything anywhere that might tell us exactly how the main rooms at the Abbey were decorated. Most of them were also re-vamped by Adam at the same time weren't they?'

'Yes that's right.' Hiding her surprise at his knowledge Brooke thought carefully. 'When I was going through my uncle's things we found an old deed box full of plans and things relating to Abbot's Meade—although the original house was built in the fifteenth century it's been extended and altered many times since then. There could be something there.'

'Where are these plans now?'

'In the loft of the Lodge.'

'Well if you've no objection I'd like to see them.'

'None at all,' Brooke assured him. Despite the informality of being on first-name terms with him, Adam, the chairman of Henderson Hart, was a very different proposition from Adam who had tried to make love to her after the cocktail party. What had she expected, she derided herself gently; that he would spend all his time chasing her round his desk? Nothing could have been further from reality. In fact she was beginning to wonder if she had dreamt the whole incident. Adam was showing her a temporary wall of filing cabinets which he explained she could organise to suit herself.

'Most of what goes into them will go into the computer as well, but until we get everything together under one roof, it will be as well to have some tangible record, especially where contracts

are concerned. I shall be spending some of my time
in London—perhaps sometimes for a couple of
days at a time. When I'm gone, I expect you to
take total charge of the office. Later on when he
arrives I'll introduce you to Tod Dearham—he's
the foreman who's going to be in charge of the
men working down here. The next time I go to
London you can come with me and I'll introduce
you to the executive staff at Head Office. Any
questions you want to ask me?'

There were only a couple of small points, which
Adam dealt with in the same speedy fashion as he
had done everything else, glancing at his watch
when he had finished to say crisply, 'Coffee time I
think—making coffee wouldn't normally be part
of your duties, but I have several 'phone calls to
make and if you don't consider the chore beneath
you, the kitchen's. . . .'

'I know where it is,' Brooke reminded him. It
had been on the tip of her tongue to tell him that
she didn't want a drink, but in the light of his own
remarks any refusal on her part to make him one
would look childish. And he had been right about
one thing. The job would be a challenge,
something she could get her teeth into and enjoy.

He was still on the 'phone when she walked
back into the library with a tray of coffee so she
left it on his desk and walked over to the terminal,
running her eyes over it and wondering how
difficult she would find it to operate. Next to it
was a word processor, and presumably this desk
would be hers. The machine was one she was
familiar with and with which she didn't anticipate
any problems, and she was just studying it, her
head bent, when she felt a prickle of awareness
sliding down her spine. As she straightened up she

realised that Adam had finished his call and that he was watching her. 'Very business-like,' he murmured, walking toward her and flicking a finger lightly across her cheek, indicating the coiled braids of her hair, 'but personally I prefer it loose.'

There were half-a-dozen cutting remarks she could have, and ought to have made—after all, hadn't this been just the sort of remark she had been tensed for from the moment she knocked on the Dower House door this morning, but strangely enough none of them came to mind. She could barely even find the impetus to move away from him. Her skin burned fierily where he had touched it and hemmed in between him and the computer equipment she was intensely aware of his body heat; of the powerfully male construction of his body beneath the elegantly tailored dark grey suit. He was looking at her mouth, and in some strange way it was almost as though he were kissing her as he had done before. A wave of heat washed dizzily over her and she almost swayed weakly towards him, but just caught herself back in time.

'Need any help with this?' His eyes left her face to study the terminal, his voice calm and concise as he explained how it worked. If she hadn't seen it with her own eyes she could never have believed that only seconds ago he had been looking at her as though he had stripped the clothes from her body and was already touching her skin; or *had* her eyes deceived her? No, she thought fiercely, wondering what sort of game he was playing with her. Not a very serious one to judge from the comments he had made to her that first night at the Lodge. Inexperienced virgins were hardly his cup of tea, and that being the case he could only be playing with her. No doubt it amused him to see the tell-tale anxiety flare to life in her eyes every time he came too close to her. Brooke wasn't a fool, despite her lack of sexual experience.

Her full mouth compressed firmly. He was playing with her with the same careless insolence of a well-fed cat towards a terrified mouse—not really wanting her but too cruel to abandon his sport. Well this mouse wasn't going to play. Straightening up she said pleasantly, 'Oh I think everything's clear to me now Adam.' The tone of her voice made him look at her and summoning all her self-confidence Brooke allowed her eyes to drift over his body in a parody of the insolent appraisal he had just given hers.

Something that could have been surprise flared briefly in his eyes and was gone. 'Tomorrow leave your hair down,' he told her in a smoky voice, watching her mockingly. 'You didn't mean it about being business-like—you did it because you knew I'd object. If you'd really wanted to be business-like you wouldn't be wearing those silk stockings.'

Fury battled with embarrassment as Brooke glared at him. She was wearing a severely tailored black suit over a cream silk blouse, and she had thought her neat court shoes and the fine black silk stockings she was wearing with them had correctly completed her outfit. Suddenly with one remark he had turned them from an unremarkable item of clothing that complemented the rest of her outfit to something teasingly erotic that she had worn to deliberately arouse him. And the worst of it was she couldn't accuse him of doing so. Snapping her teeth closed and barely restraining herself from grinding her teeth she was glad to be saved from response by the ring of the telephone.

Her first intimation that it wasn't a business call came when she heard Adam saying smoothly, 'No of course I haven't forgotten, darling. Don't worry I'll be there.'

Not wanting to eavesdrop she slipped out of the room and into the hall. It badly needed decorating—as did the entire house. Let to tenants it had been badly neglected and on several walls large patches of damp indicated how much it needed attention. From outside she could hear sounds of activity; as she stood in the hall a man walked in and smiled at her.

'Tod Dearham,' he introduced himself, 'and you must be Adam's new PA.' He grinned as he looked around. 'Never thought when the pair of us were kids that old Adam would end up with something like this. Not a penny to waste between us in those days—only difference was that Adam's mum was a widow and mine wasn't. About is he?'

'He's on the 'phone in the study,' Brooke told him, returning his smile. There was something instantly likeable about Tod Dearham; she could well imagine him as a small scruffy child, his fair hair untidy and his face streaked with dirt. It took a far greater effort of imagination to picture Adam growing up alongside him.

The library door opened and Adam stalked out. 'What the devil did you do that for?' he demanded, not seeing Tod as he turned to Brooke. 'When I want you to leave I'll let you know. . . .'

Face flaming Brooke said stiltedly, 'You seemed to be having a private conversation. . . .'

'Come on Adam,' Tod intervened grinning. 'Give the girl a chance.'

'Tod. I'm glad you're here. I want to talk to you about my plans for this place.' Adam grimaced as a loud crash came from outside. 'I'm going up to Abbot's Meade with Tod,' he told Brooke. 'Expect me back about three. Take your lunch hour while I'm gone and there's a pile of stuff on the left-hand side of my desk that needs sorting through, files making, etc.' He was gone before she could retort, leaving her to glare frustratedly after him.

In the days that followed Brooke learned to conceal from Adam just how disconcerting she found his swift metamorphosis from boss to hunter. No matter how tense or prepared she thought she was he had a knack of catching her off-guard which left *her* torn between anger and anxiety and him mockingly amused. He wanted her because he wanted to prove to her that he could have her, she thought savagely one afternoon when he had gone up to Abbot's Meade, leaving her alone in the office. She was a challenge to him, her inexperience sharpening his interest, but she was under no illusions. Even less than the other men she had disliked for the same reason, did he want her for herself. It was all a game to him and one he was only indulging in very half-heartedly with her, if the number of telephone calls he received from other women were anything to go by.

In direct contrast Brooke had found herself striking up a very pleasant friendship with Tod Dearham. She liked the natural, down-to-earth attitude of the Northerner. When she had asked him if he was married he had grinned at her and winked. 'Not yet, but I'm not saying you couldn't tempt me if you wanted to.'

She had learned from later conversations with

him that he was the eldest of a large family and suspected that one of the reasons for his single state was that he contributed a large proportion of his earnings to his family. A further discovery that surprised her was that he held a small number of shares in Henderson-Hart. Bill had been with her when she made the discovery. She had been drawing up a list of the shareholders to place in her own personal oddments file, and Bill had looked up from the papers he was studying at her small exclamation of surprise.

'Adam made them over to him,' he had told her. 'Tod is one of his oldest friends, as well as being one of the best men the company has. He's a joiner by trade and he learned the skill from his grandfather, you've only got to see Tod with an old piece of furniture or panelling to see just what it means to him. He touches it. . . .'

'Like most men touch a much-desired woman,' Adam had finished for him, walking urbanely into the room.

'Why the curiosity about Tod?' he had asked when Bill had gone. 'Not thinking of doing a bit of slumming are you?'

The jeering, hard note in his voice was unfamiliar to her and she had reacted almost instantly to it, her head coming up and her eyes blazing.

'Tod is a friend, and a person I greatly admire. That comment wasn't just insulting to me, it was insulting to him too. No one talking to him could help but be impressed by his warmth and his intelligence.'

'He comes from a hard-working, down-to-earth, working-class family,' Adam told her hardily, 'whereas you. . . .'

Anger blazed up heatedly inside Brooke. 'You're talking like someone out of a Victorian novel,' she told him furiously, 'if anyone around here has a hang-up about class it's you Adam ... I don't give a damn about what "class" Tod is supposed to come from; he's a very attractive and interesting human being.'

'Easy for you to say,' Adam derided her, hard coins of anger darkening his cheek bones, 'but then you've never seen life from the other side of the fence, have you Brooke? You've never had to see your mother being treated like dirt; slaving her life away for a pittance and supposed to be grateful for it; you've never been told that no matter what you do or how well you succeed, in some circles you're never going to be quite good enough. Nouveau riche; isn't that how people of your class describe people of mine and always with that same supercilious tone to their voices; that lifted eyebrow that conveys so much. ...'

'Perhaps once,' Brooke was forced to admit, 'but not these days; that sort of attitude is antiquated ... out of date ... these days people are assessed on their own merits, not who their antecedents were.'

That conversation lingered in her thoughts this afternoon as she worked alone. Adam had flown to the States at the beginning of the week and wouldn't be back until tomorrow. For such an urbane, sophisticated man he had an almost paranoid hang-up about the supposed class barriers.

'Something wrong?' Tod asked, suddenly walking in.

'Just thinking.'

'Umm. Not about anything pleasant by the looks of you.'

'I was thinking about Adam, actually,' she admitted, watching his smile become displaced by a frown. 'He seems to have this thing about class barriers. . . .'

'You've noticed?' Tod leaned against her desk and frowned. 'You must really have got to him then. He's normally very careful about keeping it hidden.'

'But why?' Brooke asked curiously. 'After all you and he both had similar upbringings, but you. . . .'

'I'm not the head of a multi-million pound empire,' Tod told her dryly, 'and I haven't been kicked in the teeth by a hoity-toity society bitch who thinks she's too good for me.' He saw Brooke's expression and grimaced. 'Adam would kill me if he knew what I'd just said. It was years ago now, but some things still rankle.'

'What happened?' Brooke knew she was guilty of prying and that Adam would undoubtedly be furious if he knew what she was doing, but something urged her to question Tod further. With Adam out of the office she had expected to feel more relaxed, but instead the tight coiling sensation inside her had grown. She felt restless and on edge; she wasn't sleeping properly and when she did she had the most disturbingly erotic dreams, something she had never experienced before. It didn't help knowing that Adam had featured in those dreams with her and sometimes when snatches of them came back to her during the day she would sit in front of her word processor with hot cheeks, totally unable to divert her thoughts into other channels. He was getting to her, and wouldn't he just gloat if he knew it.

Telling herself that she needed all the ammunition she could hoard, she pressed Tod to finish his story.

'It's nothing really,' he said uncomfortably, plainly wishing he had never said anything, 'but when we were kids Adam's mother worked at this big house a mile or so outside the town. It was owned by the local millowner; a local big-shot, JP, society connections, all that sort of thing. Adam used to go up there after school to do odd jobs and earn a bit of pocket money, mowing the lawns, that kind of thing.

'Well, the Delaneys had a daughter. She was away at private school most of the time, but she'd come home for the school holidays. The year he was fourteen Adam told me that when he grew up he was going to own a house bigger than the Delaneys and that he was going to marry Susan Delaney.

'I laughed at him then, the way kids do, but he must have meant it and by the time he was twenty-one he was well on his way to being richer than the Delaneys. He'd been away from Sourford for four years by then, and when he came back we could all see how much he'd changed.

'They were having some sort of charity "do" on up at the Delaneys I remember and Adam bought a ticket. It was one of these formal dress dos, and I can remember thinking how posh he looked. He'd got this new car. . . .' Tod smiled sadly and shook his head. 'I went with him, and everything was going fine until he asked Susan Delaney for a dance. She was all dolled up like the fairy off the top of a Christmas Tree and I suppose to Adam she was just as elusively tantalising and out of reach. I admired him for his guts in asking her, but she was furious. Her face just froze as she looked at him, and said in that cutting upper class voice of hers, "Dance with our cleaner's son—you must be mad."

'At least a dozen people heard her, and it went deadly quiet all around, just as it always does at the wrong moment. Adam went white. I thought he was going to kill her for a moment but he just turned on his heel and left, with me trailing behind him.'

Pity and understanding mingled in Brooke's feelings. She could well imagine Adam's hurt pride and bitter chagrin.

'What happened then?' she asked softly.

Tod shrugged. 'Oh nothing much. We went out and got drunk. . . . Five years ago I saw Susan Delaney again. She was married by then to some weak-chinned City type. Adam had been asked to give a talk at our old school. She came up to him at the reception afterwards and was all over him, I don't think I'll ever forget the expression on her face when he removed her hand from his arm and said, "I don't like being pawed by married women, Mrs Crawford." He was kinder than she'd been though. I don't think anyone overheard apart from me. He has this hang-up now about society women and in a way who can blame him? She's divorced now.'

Brooke was still thinking about Tod's revelations that night as she went home. They explained so much about Adam's personality that had puzzled her. How Susan Delaney's refusal to dance with him must have rubbed his pride raw; but surely a man of Adam's intelligence couldn't honestly believe that. . . . Sighing Brooke acknowledged to herself that emotions couldn't always be reasoned away with logic. Look at her. Against all the

inner warnings of her mind and intelligence she
was dangerously attracted to him. The way she
had listened to Tod this afternoon had brought
that home to her. Why this almost feverish need to
know everything about him that she could if she
was indifferent to him?

She missed his presence at the Dower House;
she missed the spiralling sensation of excitement
heating her veins whenever he came near her; she
missed the taunting note in his voice whenever he
said something that he knew would disturb her,
she missed him the way a woman always misses a
man who she is emotionally attached to.

Emotionally attached? In less than a month and
to a man like Adam Hart? Never, Brooke told
herself fiercely; it would be as suicidal as opening
her arteries and watching her life-blood pour out;
more so, that way would at least be relatively
painless, while loving Adam. . . . Closing her eyes
she responded to Balsebar's ecstatic welcome.

Yawning, Brooke stretched in her chair and
glanced at her watch. Just gone eleven, and she
had been on the point of going to sleep in her
chair. She got up to let Balsebar out, taking her
coffee mug to the kitchen with her as she went.
She was physically tired but her mind was over
alert; she was spending far too much time thinking
about Adam, she acknowledged with wry self-
mockery as she called Balsebar in and locked the
kitchen door.

She was just on her way upstairs when she
heard the car. By now she was familiar with the
distinctive engine note of Adam's Ferrari and her
heart leapt, blocking off her throat, her tension
increasing when she heard the car stop outside.

For a moment as she heard the gate creak she

was tempted to pretend she was already asleep. Coward, she chided herself; sooner or later she would have to face him, and it might as well be sooner.

His eyebrows rose as she opened the door before he knocked. He was dressed in a formal dark grey suit and as he stepped into the hall she could see the lines of tiredness raying out from his eyes.

'Adam, it's late,' she warned him. 'I was just on my way to bed.'

'Now there's a tantalising thought.' His mouth quirked, sexual appreciation glimmering in his eyes as he studied her. Knowing she was flushing like a schoolgirl and unable to do a thing about it Brooke headed for her sitting room.

'You said I could have those plans—the ones of Abbot's Meade,' Adam reminded her.

Her eyebrows rose. 'And you want them now? At this time of night?'

He shrugged powerful shoulders. 'Jet lag does something to my metabolism—physically I want to sleep but mentally. . . .' Again he shrugged. 'That being the case I prefer to put the time to good use.'

'They're up in the loft,' Brooke told him helplessly. 'It could take ages to find them.' A dark shape loomed into the room and walked over to Adam. He reached out a lean, tanned hand and scratched the dog's ears; the thin tail began to thump gently on the carpet. Even Balsebar wasn't proof against Adam's personality Brooke thought ruefully watching them, so how was she supposed to be?

'How about a cup of coffee for the weary traveller then?' Adam mocked. 'Or is even that too much to ask? You're quite safe Brooke,' he added in a harsher tone. 'I haven't come here bent on seduction, although the way you persist in behaving makes it a very tempting prospect at times.'

As he dropped down into one of her chairs, he surveyed her from beneath half closed eyelids, a lazily mocking smile curling his mouth as he studied her cross expression. 'Oh come on Brooke,' he drawled tautly, 'you're old enough to know the quickest way to stop a man chasing is to let him catch you. The faster you run the keener the hunter; and you've been running very fast.'

The cynicism behind his comment infuriated her. 'Now let's just get one thing straight right away,' she began angrily. 'If I've been "running" as you call it, it's because I want to put as much distance between us as I can. It's the old story isn't it Adam,' she asked fiercely, 'the old chauvinistic male idea that when a woman says "No" and he doesn't want to hear it she means "yes", well when I say "No", I mean it, I. . . .'

'Do you?' He was on his feet so quickly she didn't even have time to back away from him, brown fingers circling her wrist and closing on it until she could feel the pressure of his grip against her bones. He was angry; she could see it in his eyes, molten flecks of mercury heating the steel grey, warning her that his control was near breaking point.

'Well, let me tell you something Brooke. Your tongue might have been saying "no" loud and clear, but your body's been giving me an entirely different message. Want me to prove it to you?'

He was bitterly, almost dangerously angry; she could sense the tension building up inside him, imposing a strain which showed in his eyes and his tight muscles and for the first time she felt afraid.

'All the time I've been in the States I've been thinking about you,' he told her thickly, 'wanting you, and I don't like it Brooke. . . .'

'No, you treat the women in your life like disposable hankies don't you Adam?' she shot back at him, suddenly equally angry. 'Use them and then discard them; they all have to be kept in their place just because Susan Delaney once refused to dance with you.'

The moment the wildly angry words were out Brooke wanted to recall them, but it was too late, much, much too late.

'Damn you,' Adam swore hoarsely. 'Damn you for that Brooke,' and then his mouth was on hers fiercely bruising, taking, demanding, punishing her for her defiance and making her all too aware of her physical vulnerability to him.

'Open your mouth.' The thickly muttered command penetrated the dazed cottonwool of her brain. Brooke knew she should ignore it but something stronger than common sense seemed to have taken over, pushing her beyond logic and reason, making her want to match the bitter fury of Adam's embrace with an anger of her own; that of being made to want him against her will and judgment; of being betrayed by her own flesh; of wanting him to the point where pride and logic meant nothing and the hunger inside her for him everything.

The kiss went on and on, short-cutting a hundred conversations, giving her another, far deeper glimpse of the unsuspected sensuality of her own nature. What was it about this man, she wondered heatedly, responding blindly to the commands of his mouth and tongue, that aroused her to the point where everything else faded into insignificance?

'You want me,' Adam muttered rawly into her throat, drawing his tongue along her skin with a compulsion that left her shivering and mute with reaction. 'I can see it in your eyes, feel it in your body, you want me, and right now there isn't anything I wouldn't do to have you. You've been like a fever in my blood,' he told her half angrily, 'driving me crazy, making me ache like I haven't done since I was an adolescent. I couldn't drive past here without seeing you. I've been thinking about it ever since I got on that damned plane . . . imagining touching you like this. . . .' His hand swept over her body capturing her breast, his thumb rubbing rhythmically against the hard peak of her nipple, 'and this . . . I'll make it good for you Brooke. I'll. . . .'

His kisses were liquid fire heating her blood, the promises he moaned into her skin inflaming her senses past the point where she could control her response. She wanted him. So badly that her body shook with the force of her need. He smelled of fresh sweat and. . . . Freezing in his arms Brooke caught the scent of a rich earthy perfume where it clung to his jacket. Another woman's perfume. All at once revulsion flooded through her, sickening her almost to the point of physical nausea. She pushed Adam away, staring at him with haunted eyes and a pale face.

'What's the matter?' His voice was thick, slurred as though he found difficulty framing the words.

The sickness faded leaving in its place cold, reasoning logic. She couldn't allow Adam to become her lover; she couldn't join the long procession of other women whom he had wanted and then discarded. Better never to have known the taste of paradise than to have sipped it once and spend the rest of her life yearning to taste it again. She shivered feverishly, folding her arms round her body, her voice a faint thread of sound as she asked, 'Please leave now Adam ... I need time ... I. ...'

His fingers spread against her jaw, tilting her face up so that he could look into her eyes.

'What happened?' he demanded thickly, 'less than five minutes ago you were in my arms, responding to me ... wanting me, Brooke,' he reminded her cruelly. 'Now suddenly you're telling me you don't. Why?'

'Because you smell of another woman,' she told him simply and honestly, watching the high colour leave his face and cruel bitterness take its place.

'I've never pretended to be a monk,' he told her softly.

'No ... you haven't deceived me Adam, and I can't deceive myself. I'm not prepared to be simply one in a long line of women moving through your life.'

'Then what do you want?' he demanded savagely as he released her, stepping back from her. 'To be the only one?'

Yes, yes, her heart cried with a furious intensity that made her ache for her own pain, but she kept her face controlled and blank as she said dryly, 'I learned long ago never to hope for the impossible. Please go Adam.'

This time he didn't argue. She stood where he had left her in her small living room long after he had driven away, weak, aching, tears sliding painfully down her face, only then able to acknowledge just how much part of her had longed for him to overrule her; to stay with her and let him tutor her body in all the ways he could give it pleasure so that she could pleasure him in return.

CHAPTER FIVE

THE next day Brooke had to force herself to go to work, her nerves tensely on edge, waiting for the moment when Adam walked in through the office door and she had to face him.

When mid-morning came and went without him putting in an appearance she began to wonder if he was inflicting deliberate torment. He must know how much she was dreading coming face to face with him after last night. When he had gone she had gone to bed and then spent most of the night lying awake reminding herself of the futility of getting involved with him on a personal level—on any personal level.

When twelve o'clock came and he still hadn't appeared she couldn't stand it any longer. She could go into the kitchen and make herself a cup of coffee and if he hadn't appeared by the time it was ready she would have to go and find him.

The kettle had just boiled when she heard the kitchen door open and with a considerable effort of will she refrained from whirling round but instead poured boiling water over the dark brown grains, concentrating on her task as best she could when every one of her five senses were drawn against her will to the man she could sense watching her from the door.

'Umm, that smells good, pour me a cup will you please Brooke? You should have woken me up earlier,' she heard Adam grumble. 'It isn't often jet lag effects me like that.' He had walked up to her as he spoke and she was forced to turn and look at him. As their eyes clashed she read something in his that made her stomach churn, her body igniting with a sexual excitement that made her mind recoil in horror.

'I wonder which of us regrets my leaving last night the most Brooke?' he drawled tauntingly, watching the rich colour come and go under her pale skin, and then laughing softly as she fought not to betray any reaction to his comment. 'Fight it as hard as you like,' he murmured. 'In the end it won't make the slightest bit of difference—and you know it.'

'I won't become your sleeping partner Adam.' She said it flatly, hoping her lack of expression would reinforce her determination.

'Who said anything about sleeping?' He laughed again, the deep sound rumbling in his chest. He was wearing a loosely belted towelling robe, with nothing on beneath it probably, Brooke thought feverishly, watching him rub his hand against the dark growth of beard lining his jaw.

'You should have woken me earlier,' he complained. 'There's one hell of a lot to get through.'

'I didn't realise you were still asleep.'

'And you were too scared to come and find out? Pity, I'm sure I'd have enjoyed being woken up by you Brooke.'

Compressing her mouth Brooke handed him a mug of coffee and headed for the kitchen door.

'I think I'll take my lunch break now,' she told him crisply. 'I've left notes on your desk of all the messages I've had for you while you've been away.'

His taunting laughter followed her out into the

passage, and she virtually flew into the office, to gather up her coat and handbag. The walk back to the Lodge did much to restore her equilibrium; the cold fresh air stinging her face and easing her down on to a more level plane. What was happening to her? She shivered and knew the tremor wasn't entirely due to the fresh autumn weather. Did she have the strength to withstand Adam if he continued to pursue her? Of course she did, she told herself furiously; to think otherwise was an insult to her intelligence. She already knew exactly what Adam wanted from her and why should she find it any harder to deny him than she had found it to deny the other men who had wanted her for exactly the same reason. Adam made no pretence of wanting her for herself; of getting to know her as a person; no he simply wanted her body in his bed. She stopped abruptly, staring blindly at the Lodge. The difference was that for the first time she reciprocated a man's hunger; she wanted Adam. But she wanted more than mere sexual possession. It was enough to drive every other thought out of her head. She shivered violently, almost running up the garden path, and locking the door behind her as though she was somehow locking out her unwanted thoughts. What was she trying to tell herself? That she had 'fallen in love' with Adam. But she had never believed in 'falling in love'; at best it was a very insubstantial emotion on which to build a commitment for life, and at worst it was a state akin to madness.

Restlessly she prowled round her small kitchen, letting Balsebar out, opening the 'fridge door to remove the salad she had left prepared for her lunch and then turning away from it, knowing she could not eat.

No matter how much she denied it to him, she could not deny to herself that emotionally as well as physically she was intensely responsive to him. During his absence she had caught herself thinking about him, daydreaming stupidly over the way his hair curled over his collar at the back of his neck; of the indolent way he moved when he was at his most dangerously perceptive; the way he smiled and frowned.

By the time her lunch hour was up she had managed to regain some slight composure. It ought to have helped to discover that in her absence Adam had gone out, but instead of finding it easier to settle down to work she found it harder. Where was he? She punched restlessly at the computer keyboard, staring at the screen without really seeing it, her tense nerves only relaxing when she heard the unmistakable purr of the Ferrari.

She was ready for Adam's entrance, head bent studiously over her work, determined not to react to him; what she wasn't prepared for was the light, feminine voice that drawled disdainfully, 'This is your office? Really Adam darling, I thought you'd come up in the world.'

The voice was the type that always made her bristle; far too obviously 'upper class', hinting at an artificiality that grated.

'Susan, let me introduce you to my PA, Brooke Beauclere.'

Adam's voice, deep and richly toned, soothed her raw nerves, until they picked up on the woman's name. Telling herself that she was jumping to ridiculous conclusions Brooke stood up and turned round.

The blonde woman she found herself face to face with confirmed the mental image she had

built up of her from her voice. Everything about
her was artificial Brooke thought distastefully,
from her too-carefully applied make-up to her
obviously expensive and highly fashionable outfit.
Her blonde hair was cleverly streaked, her skin
so smooth that Brooke found herself wondering
cynically if its flawless tautness was entirely
natural. Despite her slender figure and youthful
demeanour Brooke knew she was probably
somewhere in her mid-thirties. Her eyes betrayed
it. They were the eyes of a woman used to
hunting down her prey and keeping it, and right
now they were most definitely warning Brooke
off Adam.

'Miss Beauclere.'

Her voice was icy cold and if anything even
more deliberately 'top drawer'. Brooke itched to
let her own antagonism show in response, but
pride prevented her from letting Adam see just
how much he had undermined her defences.
Keeping her smile warm and her voice as light as
she could, she responded cheerfully.

Just for a moment she thought she saw unholy
amusement glint in Adam's eyes as his companion
absorbed all the information Brooke's voice and
manner relayed to her, and then he said casually,
'Brooke's family owned Abbot's Meade until quite
recently.'

The other woman was shocked, but she hid it
well, smiling venomously at Brooke and saying
sweetly, 'That's the trouble with these old places,
isn't it? So many businessmen buy them without
realising just how costly they are to run. I suppose
it's no wonder that they're passing out of the
hands of the original owners. How long had your
family owned it?'

Her voice implied that it couldn't have been very long. She was being quite deliberately put in her place, Brooke recognised, accepting the snub with a grim smile, only just concealing her astonishment when Adam said smoothly, 'Oh, since fifteen hundred and odd, give or take a generation or so, isn't that right, Brooke?'

Susan looked furious, hard, angry colour flushing her cheek bones. As a young girl she must have been exquisite, Brooke recognised, but now she possessed a hardness that she personally found chilling. She struck Brooke as the type of woman who put a price on everything. It seemed that Adam had found a kindred spirit, she decided cynically, glancing towards the door as it opened and Tod walked in.

'Well, well,' he grinned, 'if it isn't lady Susan. What brings you out slumming my lady?'

'I don't think that's particularly funny.' She fixed him with a freezing glare and then said coldly to Adam. 'Really Adam I should have thought by now you'd have taught your staff to have a little more respect. . . .'

'You seem to forget that Tod and I grew up together.'

'Yes well. . . .' For a moment she looked slightly uncomfortable, and Brooke knew with a sinking sensation that her earlier misgivings were right. His companion was the woman who had so cruelly rejected Adam. So what was she doing here with him; the two of them apparently on the very best of terms?

'It was good of you to give me lunch darling,' Susan made a play of smoothing down the skirt of her suit, 'but I really must fly now. I only popped down here out of curiosity really. Having read so much about you in the press recently, and as we're such old . . . friends. . . .'

Behind her back Tod grimaced slightly in Brooke's direction and Adam, who was facing them, picked up the exchange, his eyes darkening warningly as he said smoothly to Susan. 'Any time Sue. I'll see you out to your car.'

When they were safely out of the room Tod frowned after them. 'That one's got all the hunting instincts of a killer shark. I suppose she's hoping to make Adam husband number two.'

'After the way she rejected him?' Brooke was shocked and let it show, 'But surely Adam. . . .'

'Adam's only human like everyone else,' Tod reminded her wryly, 'and remember he's probably not seeing her as a thirty-odd-year-old woman on the look out for a second rich husband to keep her in the style to which she's grown accustomed, but as an eighteen-year-old girl who he put up on a pedestal.'

It was an extremely sobering thought and one that haunted Brooke all through the afternoon. Every now and then she stopped work, and watched Adam, feeling the sensation of pain and loss building up inside her and unable to do a thing about it. She hadn't realised that he had seen her until he commented sardonically, 'What's the matter? Have I suddenly grown two heads?'

She turned her back to him, not trusting herself to respond to him, glad when five-thirty came and she could reasonably make her escape.

Back at the Lodge she sat down with her supper and tried to analyse her feelings. She had been jealous of Susan, searingly, bitterly jealous; the feeling such an alien one to her that it had taken her several minutes to recognise it. Her instant antipathy towards the other woman had surprised her with its intensity, and she felt a renewal of her earlier stomach churning nausea as she remembered how she had reacted.

This madness had to stop. She had no intention of becoming just one more name in the long list of Adam's bedmates, and what else was there for her? A lifetime working as his devoted assistant; sharing his working hours and yet constantly having to tame and subdue all her physical responses to him; knowing that he would be spending his nights with other, more amenable women; women who he could use and then pay off when he grew bored with them?

Not even a brisk walk with Balsebar managed to drive out her preoccupation with him, and she returned to the Lodge, grateful that the weekend was looming and that she would have a brief respite in which to re-charge her batteries.

In the event the respite came sooner than she had envisaged, and was far from pleasant. When she arrived at work the following day Adam told her that he had business in London which would take him away all day. He looked preoccupied and tense and there was none of the sexual speculation in his scrutiny of her that she had grown used to seeing.

He didn't come back that night, but on the Saturday as Brooke returned from shopping she saw the Ferrari turn in through the gates, and Adam wasn't alone. As she recognised the blonde hair of his companion Brooke felt her stomach lurch with sickness. It was a cold dismal day, and with the encroaching evening came the heavy rain which had been threatening all day. Brooke let Balsebar out as usual whilst she prepared his evening meal but when she went to call him in there was no sign of the Afghan. An icy, stinging wind lashed the rain against her skin as she stood by the open door, and her heart sank. Balsebar occasionally did this, taking it into his head to be awkward, but she couldn't allow him to roam all evening. He had precious little road sense and could easily wander through the grounds on to the main road. At the thought of her pet lying maimed or dead, hit by some motorist, her stomach lurched again, and without bothering to do more than pick up his lead and a torch Brooke hurried out into the wet night.

An hour later, her throat hoarse from calling him, she admitted defeat. She had gone through fear to anger and back to stomach churning fear again as she searched the grounds.

After towelling her soaking hair and changing into dry clothes she was just about to pick up the 'phone and ring the police when she heard a knock on her door.

Tense with apprehension she hurried to open it, staring at the last person she had expected to see there, her soft, 'Adam ...' doing nothing to lighten his grim expression.

'Is something wrong?'

'It's that damned dog of yours,' he told her impatiently. 'He's howling his head off in the study, and refusing to leave. You'd better come and collect him.'

Just for a moment she was almost sick with relief. What on earth was Balsebar doing at the Dower House?

'What the hell's he doing out on a night like this anyway?' Adam growled.

'He ran off. I've just been out looking for him.'

'You shouldn't keep a dog if you aren't prepared to see that he's properly trained. Come on,' he demanded brusquely. 'I've got dinner guests waiting for me. . . . The Ferrari's outside, get in.'

He sounded so angry and distant that Brooke didn't dare ask him if she could go and get a coat. Despite her dry clothes she was cold and she shivered as she followed him outside.

They drove to the Dower House in a grim silence, Brooke following Adam in through the kitchen where a couple of women she recognised from the village were busy with preparations for his dinner party. She had heard Balsebar's howls the moment she opened the car door, and her heart sank as she saw Adam's furiously angry expression.

'I'm sorry about this Adam.' To her dismay her voice quivered faintly, but he didn't seem to hear her, striding through the hall and flinging open the study door.

The moment she walked into the room Balsebar stopped howling and began instead an award-worthy performance of a grovelling and distraught offender. As Brooke slipped his lead on, the study door opened and Susan walked in. She was wearing a crimson silk cocktail dress, diamonds glinting in her ears, her face hard and angry.

The moment he saw her Balsebar tensed, growling softly, a look of mutual antipathy passing between woman and dog. 'Please hurry up and get that animal out of here,' she told Brooke imperiously. 'Adam, my parents can hardly hear one another speak over the row that animal's been making. How on earth did he get into the grounds in the first place? You ought to hire a keeper.

Daddy has one. He has instructions to shoot trespassing strays. They're a menace to the stock. . . .'

Too furious to care what she said Brooke whipped round, her face white with temper and strain. 'In case you haven't noticed, Abbot's Meade doesn't have any stock,' she said curtly, 'and you must remember that it was, until recently, Balsebar's home.'

'But it isn't now, is it?' Susan returned bitingly, adding so that only Brooke could hear her. 'Perhaps that's something you should *both* remember,' before she turned and stalked out of the room.

Adam, who had been studying some papers on his desk, turned to her and said coolly, 'Susan has a point, Brooke. I can't have Balsebar running tame in the Park. It isn't as though. . . .'

'It's his home any more? Yes, I do realise that. . . .' Feeling almost light-headed with temper and stress, Brooke walked blindly out of the room, ignoring the sound of Adam's voice behind her. Only instinct led her to the front door; her eyes were too full of angry tears for her to see where she was going. Outside the wind whipped them away, Adam's angry demand for her to come back following her as she turned and said brightly, 'Please don't let me keep you from your guests Adam. . . . Balsebar and I can make our own way back . . . and I'll make sure that neither of us has to disturb you like this again.'

By the time she reached the Lodge she was crying in earnest, but the high, keening sound of the wind was whipping the sound away, her face as wet from the rain as it was from her tears. Once inside she dried the dog with an old towel she kept expressly for that purpose and then fed him. For once he seemed almost dejected and kept nuzzling her with his long pointed nose, his eyes sad and knowing. 'What on earth am I going to do with you?' she asked him softly, rubbing his ears and stifling the sneeze suddenly tickling the back of her nose. She was frozen, she realised, shivering as she reached to turn and throw more logs on the fire.

By Sunday Brooke knew she was in for a bad cold. Sunday night found her shivering and hugging the fire, alternately sneezing and coughing. On Monday morning she felt too ill to go to work but went anyway. She was just uncovering her typewriter when Adam walked in and announced abruptly, 'Leave that—I've got to go to London and you're coming with me. We'll be there for several days, so you'd better go back to the Lodge and pack what you need.'

'I can't go with you.' Brooke forced back a sneeze and turned to face him. Adam's eyebrows lifted, signifying his impatience.

'Why not? It's part of your contract,' he reminded her crisply. 'You won't be much use to me as my PA if you can't work away from here when I want you to.'

'I have a dog—remember?' she asked sardonically.

'I'll get Tod to feed and exercise him for you. I need you with me Brooke,' he told her curtly. 'There's a problem with one of our major contracts—we're on a time penalty clause with it, and apart from the loss of prestige if it goes wrong we can't afford to risk losing money by paying out on penalty clauses. I don't want to trip up on this one. Susan's father is watching our progress on it with a sharp eye—if all goes well we could be asked to tender for some work for his company. . . . That's why they were here the other night. Susan had suggested he might talk to me. . . .'

'Big of him.' Brooke muttered through her teeth, unaware that Adam had heard her until he walked over to her desk and turned her round, watching her. The touch of his hands on her shoulders light though it was seemed to burn right through her clothes. She had felt cold on coming into the room; now she felt extremely hot.

'And what exactly did that little crack mean?' His voice was so soft she had difficulty in catching the words, but his eyes were inimical, cold and searching as they studied her flushed face. A huge sneeze defeated her efforts to control it, and Brooke pushed away from him, diving for her handkerchief.

'Are you all right?'

'Just a bit of a cold,' Brooke lied. She was far from 'all right', but suddenly she wanted to go to London with him; she wanted to be with him even if it was only as his secretary.

They left just over an hour later, Tod having been introduced to Balsebar who accepted his overtures of friendship with regal decorum.

'I'm sorry he interrupted your dinner party the other night,' Brooke apologised as they sped through the Lodge gates.

'And I'm sorry I blew up at you the way I did, but it was a rather fraught day.'

'Yes, I can understand why.'

'You can?' A sharp look accompanied his words. 'How so?'

Knowing that she had said too much, Brooke bit her lip, refusing to say any more.

There was a moment's silence before Adam said. 'I see. . . .' And then a rather enigmatic smile curved his mouth making Brooke itch to know what had caused it.

'You look sleepy,' he told her, interrupting her train of thought. 'Why don't you try and rest?'

Before leaving the Lodge she had taken a rather large dose of a liquid cold remedy, and it was beginning to make her feel extremely light-headed. The heat of the car added to her torpor and it was easier to lean back in her seat and close her eyes, than to argue.

The next thing Brooke knew was that Adam was shaking her awake, concern, and something approaching anger darkening his eyes as hers opened reluctantly. The interior of the car was in darkness and for a moment Brooke felt totally disorientated. 'What time is it?' she asked huskily, sneezing and then shivering, as she looked hesitantly at the darkness outside. Could it be evening already? Could she really have slept that long.

'Just gone twelve,' Adam told her, adding curtly, 'Why the hell didn't you tell me you weren't well.'

'It's only a cold. . . .'

'Cold or not, you're in no fit state to wwork. Come on.' He opened the car door, walking round to her side while she was still struggling with her seat belt to open her door for her and then retrieve their cases from the boot.

'Over there.' He nodded, indicating a lift, and Brooke realised that they were in an underground car park. As Adam followed her into the lift, he pressed the bell and they rose smoothly and extremely swiftly upwards. When the lift doors finally opened Brooke was dazzled by the gleaming white foyer she found herself in. Everything was stark and white, with the exception of the massed plants in one corner.

The foyer was small and empty, only one door leading off it. The silence unnerved her. Where were they?

'My apartment,' Adam told her, obviously reading her mind, as he punched a series of numbers into a complicated lock system.

'You'll be staying here while we're in London.' The look he gave her was coolly disparaging. 'Not that you'll be doing much work today. That way,' he told her when she simply stood where she was, almost struck dumb by what he was saying. 'What are you waiting for?' he asked her grimly. 'Surely not to be carried over the threshold?'

Brooke went white. 'I can't stay *here*.' Even in her own ears her voice sounded husky with panic. 'I thought we'd be staying in an hotel. I. . . .'

'When I'm already paying an extortionate rent for this place?' Adam laughed harshly, and then said crisply. 'Stop looking at me like that Brooke, I didn't bring you here to seduce you if that's what's worrying you. In fact I wouldn't have brought you at all if I'd guessed how ill you are,' he told her callously. 'Why the hell didn't you say you weren't feeling well.'

Why hadn't she done? Because she hadn't been able to bear the thought of knowing he was in London, and yet not knowing what he was doing . . . who he was seeing.

'It's only a cold,' she told him unconvincingly, 'I'll be all right in. . . .' Even as she spoke she felt the sudden tidal wave of weakness roll over her, taking her completely off guard. The room turned black, the floor heaving and bucking. She must have made a faint cry because she heard Adam swear and then nothing.

Her last conscious thought was that Adam must be furious with her and that she couldn't possibly have seen concern for her in his eyes in those last few seconds of consciousness.

CHAPTER SIX

SHE was so hot, Brooke thought fretfully, plucking restlessly at the bedclothes ... far far too hot, and what was she doing in bed on such a hot day? As she struggled to sit up and push away the constricting bedclothes, she realised that she was wrapped up in them like a mummy, and that, for some reaon, trying to extricate herself from them was proving to be a herculean task.

'Oh no, you don't.... It took me twenty minutes to get you wrapped up in those.'

Firm male fingers pushed away her hands, tugging back the detested bedclothes, the familiar voice suddenly increasing her weakness. Adam ... but what was he doing here? For the first time Brooke became aware of the unfamiliarity of her surroundings. This bedroom decorated in rich creams and bronzes wasn't her room.

'Adam?' Her voice croaked over his name, startling her with its husky dryness. Her throat felt sore, and a feeling of inexplicable panic washed over her. She felt so weak and helpless.

'Drink this.' The glass of barley water Adam produced was soothingly refreshing, once she had got over the shock of having him hold both it and the back of her neck while she drank, the deftness of his movements suggesting that it was a service he had performed many, many times.

'Lie down again now Brooke. The doctor said you were to get as much rest as you could. Why didn't you tell me you weren't feeling well before we left Abbot's Meade?'

Abbot's Meade. Suddenly everything came rushing back, and Brooke remembered how ill she had felt in the car on the way to London and how she had striven to hide it from Adam, not wanting to be left behind while he. . . . She risked a glance at his face and wished she had not done so when she saw how bitterly angry he looked.

'I should be at work,' she protested huskily. 'I shouldn't be. . . .'

'At work?' He laughed harshly. 'Just what are you trying to do to me? Turn me into a complete ogre. You've come dangerously close to pneumonia. For a couple of nights it was touch and go whether you ought to be admitted into hospital.'

A couple of nights. Then how long had she been here? Brooke stared mutely at him for several seconds before voicing the question.

'Five days.' Adam told her brusquely, adding mockingly, and before you ask the next question. '*I* have . . .'

'*You* have what?' Brooke asked him dryly, knowing exactly what he meant but needing to hear it put into words before she could comprehend the full humiliation of her position.

'*I* have looked after you,' Adam told her.

'But your work. . . . You should have sent me home. . . .'

She watched the way his mouth twisted. 'To that cold, damp cottage with no one to look after you?' He shook his head, his face unexpectedly bleak. 'You've been very ill Brooke, and to some extent that's my fault. You rambled a good deal,' he told her tersely, and Brooke was thankful that he turned from her to the curtained window. What had she said? That she loved him? Dear God, surely not that. 'In your fever you re-lived your search for that damned dog. . . .'

Relief flooded through her body. 'But Adam that was hardly your fault. . . .'

'It was my fault that I didn't realise the state you were in when you collected him.' Long fingers drummed impatiently on a small table. 'My doctor tells me that you've probably been overdoing things for some time.' He frowned. 'I hadn't realised you'd been nursing your uncle for quite so long. . . .'

He had been doing some digging Brooke thought resentfully, unless of course that was something else she had told him during her fever.

'You didn't need to look after me yourself,' she blurted out, angry with herself when her skin coloured up under his sharp look. 'I mean . . . I know how busy you are . . . You could have hired a nurse. . . .'

'Could *you* have afforded it?' he mocked unkindly. 'No, it was something I had to do Brooke. Call it a penance if you like. . . .' Outside the bedroom door a 'phone rang, and Adam swore impatiently, 'I'd better go and answer that. You stay right where you are.'

When he had gone Brooke forced herself to try and relax. Without Adam's presence she was acutely aware of how weak she felt and she closed her eyes, snatches of memory filtering back. She remembered waking up shivering and being soothed back to sleep by a touch she had thought was her father's, but which she knew now must have been Adam's. Beneath the bedclothes she suddenly realised that she wasn't wearing anything, and her body flamed hotly. She was just trying to come to terms with the implication of this discovery when Adam re-appeared, walking quickly to her side to rest cool fingers on her forehead.

'You look flushed,' he told her, frowning. 'I hope your temperature isn't up again.'

'No ... no, I'm fine.' Agitatedly Brooke pushed him away. 'I'd like to go to the bathroom. If. ... Adam what are you doing,' she protested, quivering with shock as he thrust back the bedclothes and picked her up.

'You said you wanted to go to the bathroom,' he told her mildly, 'I'm taking you there. ...'

'No ... please. ...' How could she explain to him that her request had stemmed from an urgent need to escape from him? 'I can walk there ... please put me down.'

He did as she asked, but before she could give vent to the sigh of relief trembling on her lips, he sat down on the bed beside her; an extremely large bed Brooke now realised, like the room it was in, which was surely no mere guest room. Her heartbeat seemed to accelerate tenfold in the few seconds it took Adam to start talking; she felt sure he must be able to see it thumping beneath the cotton sheet he had wrapped her in.

'Now let's get one thing straight,' he said calmly. 'You're shrinking away from me as though you're expecting me to pounce on you and commit instant rape. If that was what I wanted I could have had my evil way with you any time during these last five days. ...'

'It's not that. ...' Hastily Brooke avoided his eyes. Adam would never need to stoop to rape—far from it.

'Then what is it?' A smile suddenly tugged at the

corners of his mouth as she clutched the sheet even closer to her body. 'Ah so that's it,' he murmured softly. 'Well, it's far too late for embarrassment now Brooke, I know your body almost as intimately as I know my own. . . .'

He saw the rich colour storming up under her skin, and frowned, dropping his bantering manner. 'It was all extremely clinical I assure you, I did only what I would have done for anyone else in the same circumstances—male or female. . . .'

'You could have hired a nurse . . . asked one of the other secretaries. . . .'

'Perhaps, but I thought you'd find it embarrassing going back to work afterwards. You and I know your presence here is quite innocent, but. . . .'

'No matter how innocent I might be, no one would believe it once they knew I'd been staying with you,' Brooke finished bitterly for him. 'Knowing that, why did you bring me here in the first place?'

A smile teased the corners of his mouth, 'Ah . . . now this is where I believe I plead the fifth amendment.' He smiled at her, and Brooke knew that he meant that he had intended to make love to her and that was why he had brought her to his apartment instead of booking her into an hotel. Of course he wouldn't want his other employees to know he was having an affair—no matter how brief—with a mere PA. It would be bad for morale—the remainder of the female staff would probably be queueing up for their turn instead of concentrating on their work, she thought cynically.

'Well now that I'm recovered, I think I ought to leave. . . .'

'*If* you were recovered I might agree with you,' Adam agreed calmly, 'but you're not. And that isn't just my view, it's Doctor Peters' as well. He's been extremely concerned about you Brooke.' For a moment, as he turned his head away from her, in profile there seemed to be a tension etched into his features she hadn't seen before, the bones of his face faintly gaunt and stressed.

'Adam I can't continue to stay here now. . . .' Brooke protested, avoiding looking at him. 'Staying in your apartment. . . .'

'Sharing my bed,' he mocked, laughing at her. 'Is that what you were going to say? I assure you that for once my motives were totally pure. It made more sense to sleep here with you where I could keep a check on you than put you in another room and keep having to get up. You're an extremely restless sleeper, do you know that?'

He saw the doubt shimmering in her eyes and reached for her, grasping her shoulders, pulling her up into a sitting position facing him. The sheet which had become slightly loose started to slip, but as Brooke made a grab for it, Adam shook her, stopping her. 'Leave it,' he told her curtly. 'You're forgetting I've seen it all already, and Brooke . . . if and when I do make love to you, you'll be fully conscious of every second of it.' For a moment he looked extremely bitter, and then his expression changed as he said lazily, 'You really are the most provoking female, you know. Doctor Peters is coming in later. I've given him a key. I've got to go into the office for a while this morning, but no trying to convince him that you're fully recovered because you'll be wasting your time.'

Later in the morning the doctor arrived as Adam had told her. A small, balding man in his

late fifties he gave Brooke a thorough examina-
tion, tutting frowningly as he did so.

'You're an extremely lucky young woman,' he
told her firmly when he had finished. 'You came
very close to being very ill. You've been overdoing
things my girl, and what you need. . . .' He broke
off, turning to the door as it opened and Adam
walked in.

'Is our patient giving you any trouble doctor?'
he asked watching the colour come and go in
Brooke's face. She was sure that the doctor
thought she was Adam's girlfriend—how could he
think otherwise when she was here in his bed?

'I have just been telling her what a very lucky
girl she is,' the doctor told him. 'What she needs
now is a few more days' rest and then a good
holiday. . . .' He got up, smiling down at Brooke.
'Now, you aren't to even think of getting up for
another two days at least, and then just for a few
hours at a time. . . .'

The two men walked out of the room and
Brooke could hear them talking, discussing her no
doubt. Their voices grew fainter and then she
heard a door opening and closing. Five minutes
later Adam walked back into the room, carrying a
tray.

'Mrs Benson's home-made chicken soup,' he
told her. 'Mrs Benson is my "daily" by the
way. . . .'

'And I suppose she thinks I'm your latest
woman as well,' Brooke burst out bitterly, unable
to keep the accusation back.

'Too? Meaning that so does the good doctor?'
Adam arched his eyebrows, 'Now do you
understand why I chose to involve as few people
as possible in your care?'

'You could have employed a nurse . . . someone who would have been totally outside the company. . . .'

'Nurses have friends,' he told her blandly, 'and while I hate to sound boastful, my private life does tend to come under scrutiny from the newshounds. Believe me Brooke I had no intention of embarrassing you by looking after you, I simply thought it would prevent the sort of publicity I'm sure you'd hate. . . .'

'The sort of publicity that Susan wouldn't like either,' Brooke stormed angrily, watching his eyes narrow and darken slightly.

'Perhaps not,' he agreed carefully, not giving anything away, and reaching behind her to plump up her pillows. 'Come on, try this soup, it's delicious. . . .'

He refused to let her talk any more, feeding her the soup in small spoonfuls. Brooke wanted to protest that she wasn't a baby and that she could feed herself but somehow she knew that Adam would overrule her.

'Tomorrow if you're a very good girl I might let you have a bath,' he teased her when she had eaten enough to satisfy him. He laughed when he saw the alarm leaping to life in her eyes. 'Don't worry, Mrs Benson will help you. She is someone we can trust. . . .'

'You mean she doesn't gossip about your women,' Brooke replied bitterly.

Adam put down the bowl and lifted the tray off the bed. 'Why does the thought of being thought of as one of my "women" offend you so much?' he asked conversationally, 'I assure you they are all renowned for their beauty and. . . .'

'I know what they're renowned for,' Brooke

snapped back, 'and I don't want to be classed among them. . . .'

In her heart of hearts she knew that what she really wanted was to be his only woman, but Adam seemed to lose patience with her and snarled back angrily, 'Don't worry, you're hardly likely to be, with your lack of experience.'

His condemnation hurt and she flinched back from the rebuke, knowing that it was richly deserved and yet unable to stop herself from feeling pain. She started to tremble and heard Adam curse. 'You're shivering,' he told her almost accusingly. 'Are you too hot? Too cold?' His fingers brushed her skin, busily tugging her protective sheet more closely round her. The fact that he could be so little affected by their proximity while she was having difficulty in controlling her heart-beat and pulse rate infuriated her. 'Why do I have to wear this . . .' she demanded shrilly. 'Why can't I wear my night-dress?'

'Because, my little spitfire, there's only so much that mere man can stand, and after one night of having you cuddle up to me wearing that frivolous piece of silk and lace you are pleased to describe as "nightwear", I decided for both our sakes, something more protective was called for, hence the sheet.'

During his speech Brooke's face had gone from pink to white and back to deep pink again.

'I didn't . . .' she protested huskily, 'I. . . .'

'I assure you that you did,' Adam told her mock solemnly, unable to stop his eyes from gleaming slate grey with amusement as he watched her, 'and extremely delightful it was too. I had to forcibly remind myself that you were ill. You're a very enticing female indeed, when you forget to be so prim and proper, but then, I've always known you would be.'

'I didn't know what I was doing. . . .' Even to her own ears her voice sounded strangely uncertain.

'Then it's just as well that I did, isn't it?' Adam's voice had changed again, sounding harsh this time.

'I've got to get back to the office,' he told her curtly. 'I'll be back later this evening.'

When he was gone, from somewhere Brooke managed to find the energy to remove herself from his bed into another one in one of the two spare rooms. The bed felt cold and alien, and she missed the indefinable but comforting masculine scent of him which had permeated the other room.

When he returned and found her there Adam made no comment, apart from looking at her rather grimly and that night as she lay sleepless staring at the ceiling, Brooke fought against her longing to be with him. It was bad enough that she loved him; there was no point in compounding her misery by adding the torment of knowing his lovemaking only to lose it.

Three days later Dr Peters called and pronounced that Brooke was well enough to be allowed up for a few hours that evening. A rapport had sprung up between her and Mrs Benson, who far from being the disapproving dragon Brooke had envisaged, turned out to be a softly spoken Scot in her mid forties who clucked sympathetically over Brooke, and coaxed her to eat her wonderful home-made dishes.

'As bad as Mr Hart you are,' she complained disapprovingly when Brooke only ate a few mouthfuls of the cottage pie she had made her for lunch. 'Only with him it's that he doesn't get time to eat more than a few bites.'

Her comment increased the feelings of guilt that had been tormenting Brooke for the last few days. She ought to be working; or at the very least recuperating out of Adam's way, instead of taking up so much of his time. She had wondered why they didn't return to Abbot's Meade, until Dr Peters had unwittingly answered her unspoken question by telling her that during the early days of her illness he had wanted her where she could be rushed into hospital if the need had arisen. 'Touch and go' was how he had described her condition and Brooke winced when he lectured her on looking after herself properly.

Adam must think her every kind of fool; she knew he was fed up with the present situation; he barely spoke to her when he came home now, and often it was gone eight before he did return, spending hardly more than five minutes in her room before leaving.

No doubt he was finding it irksome having her constantly underfoot; Adam was a sensual, virile man, and there could hardly have been many nights in the past that he had spent alone, never mind close on two weeks. The thought made her go hot and cold with a desire that was daily growing almost out of control. She loved Adam and she wanted him; so badly that at times she came close to almost begging him to make love to her. Only the sturdy common sense she had always prided herself on stopped her; only the knowledge that after the blissful delirium of being with him would come the empty wastelands of being without him. At least this way she would have some of him, working closely with him, perhaps establishing a friendship which would, in the end, last far longer than mere sexual desire. Because she could not deceive herself. No matter how intense or deep her love for Adam, he could only reciprocate with physical desire, and she already knew that it would not be enough.

Sighing, Brooke got up and headed for her bathroom. Dr Peters had said she could get up and she might as well do so. In fact she felt so much better than she had expected when she was bathed and dressed that she decided now was the time to tackle Adam about her return to Abbot's Meade. She couldn't continue where she was much longer without betraying how she felt about him.

At six o'clock Mrs Benson left, telling Brooke that she had left a meal prepared in the 'fridge. 'It only needs heating up,' she told Brooke as she let herself out.

Eight o'clock came and went and Brooke, who had been sitting on the leather settee in the living room, stretched her tense limbs and tried to concentrate on the television programme she was watching, all the while conscious of the storm of butterflies hovering in her tummy.

By half-past eight she was so tense that she could feel the uneven thud of her own heart beat, as she battled against the physical exhaustion undermining her determination to stay awake.

She couldn't stay here any longer; the more she thought about it, the more determined she was that she must leave, but despite her determination to stay awake, it became impossible to keep her eyes open. Her body still not recovered from her illness clamoured for sleep, the television screen flickering unwatched as Brooke gave in to it.

'Brooke, are you all right?'

The anxiety in Adam's voice pierced through the veils of sleep and Brooke opened her eyes, struggling to sit up and collapsing back against the cushions, wincing from the cramp pains suddenly stabbing through her ankle.

'What is it. . . . What's wrong?' Adam flung off his raincoat as he dropped down beside her, his forehead creased in concern. 'Dr Peters warned you not to overdo things. . . .'

'It's cramp in my ankle, that's all,' Brooke managed to tell him breathlessly, suddenly, yearningly aware of him. His skin smelled of cold, fresh air; and it must have been raining because his hair was slightly damp. She longed to reach out and touch it, to smooth her fingers through the thick dark strands. 'Here, let me. . . .' he pushed away her fingers as they reached towards her ankle, his own firmly soothing the tense mucles, massaging them into releasing her from the clamping pain, only it wasn't merely release she felt, it was a wild, sweet aching that spread from his fingers all along her body, making it tremble with need and excitement.

She had dressed comfortably in a soft wool jumper and a matching pleated skirt and beneath the jumper she could feel her breasts tingling with aching life. Her whole body seemed to be awash with sensation and she closed her eyes as she fought against it. If the mere touch of his fingers against her skin could affect her like this how would she feel if. . . .

'Brooke.'

At the sharp anxiety in his voice her eyes flew open, unwittingly revealing her response to him as he looked down at her. Instantly his own eyes narrowed, darkening stormily. 'Brooke.' This time he said her name thickly, slowly.

Aware of the danger she was courting, Brooke struggled to sit up and pull away from him. 'Adam, I must leave here,' she told him nervously. 'You're far too busy for me to be taking up more of your time. I. . . .' She made the mistake of glancing at him, her glance caught by the hard male outline of his mouth, curving in a grim line of comprehension. Her stomach lurched protestingly as she watched, mesmerised. Her own lips suddenly felt dry and she touched them lightly with her tongue, shivering with a tension that had nothing to do with the room temperature. More than anything else in the world she wanted the feel and taste of Adam's mouth against her own; she wanted to know the possession of those hard male lips, to feel. . . . She closed her eyes, reeling with the shock of her own emotions; with the depth of her hunger and the shameless wantonness of it.

Adam misinterpreted her action and leaned over her, fingers curling into her shoulders. 'Brooke, don't faint on me now.' Brooke heard him command. 'Dr Peters says you aren't well enough to fend for yourself yet. You heard him, you need a holiday. . . .'

She opened her eyes, intending to argue with him and found he was so close that she could see the pores of his skin; smell the intimate male scent that was his alone. Almost instinctively she swayed towards him, trapped in the sensual burst of pleasure his proximity gave her. She could feel the fierce thud of his heart and the heat coming off his skin beneath his jacket and shirt. His fingers bit into her shoulders as he supported her, and beneath the healthy colour of his tan, his skin seemed to pale and tighten over his bones, a febrile glitter darkening his eyes.

'The way you're looking at me would tempt a saint,' he muttered rawly, watching her, 'and that's something I've never claimed to be. God knows I shouldn't be doing this.' He made to pull away and Brooke's heart leaped in sharp dread. He couldn't leave her now. Her hands locked behind his neck, her face upturned towards him.

'Brooke. . . .' Her name was a groan of despair on his lips, lost as they found the parted sweetness of hers. A wild feverish pleasure coursed through her as Brooke responded mindlessly to his kiss, fuelling the fires she could sense burning inside him. All the advice she had given herself was forgotten as she returned his kisses abandonedly, wanting only to take what she could; to live only for the moment. All her barriers were down; her fierce response to Adam's kiss burning away all restraint. His hands moved from her shoulders down over her body, moulding and exploring, enticing her to arch wantonly against him. The hard pressure of his mouth increased, his tongue investigating the recesses of her mouth. Brooke ached with need and pleasure. She wanted to be close to him without the barrriers of their clothes. Her fingers tugged almost blindly at the buttons on his shirt, and she heard his half-stifled groan, her famished senses relishing the deep intensity of it, half of her registering his muttered, 'Yes . . . yes . . . I need to be close to you Brooke,' while the other urged her to hurry, her skin on fire for the soothing balm of his. She shivered in hectic excitement when he removed her jumper, her skirt soon following it on to the floor. She had managed to unfasten half the buttons on his shirt, but Adam completed the task for her, wrenching impatiently at them and then discarding both shirt and jacket. His torso gleamed softly gold in the lamplight and Brooke shivered again, mesmerised by the male beauty of him, reaching out to touch him with trembling fingers, lost in a tactile voyage of discovery, emotion after emotion chasing one another across her pale face as she touched and explored the hard shape of his shoulders. A pulse thudded erratically in his throat and she touched that too, with one finger, feeling the hurried thud of his life blood and wondering at her ability to increase it. She felt him swallow through rigid throat muscles and looked into his face, barely recognising the look she saw there. Adam, who was always so calm and controlled, was looking at her with a darkly intense hunger, wanting her so badly she could see his need.

Shivers of fire ran over her skin, her heart thudding in time to his pulse as she lifted her head and placed her lips against his throat, shuddering in reaction to Adam's thickly muttered cry of pleasure. His thumbs stroked the soft curve of flesh exposed by the lace cups of her bra, and Brooke thought she heard him mutter, 'this is complete madness', before he reached behind her, unsnapping it, his palms warm as they cupped her breasts, warmth turning to liquid heat as the pads of his thumbs rubbed erotically over her hard nipples. Heat, liquid, fiery waves of it submerged every other thought, her body responding feverishly to his touch, her lips scattering tiny kisses against his skin as Adam's hands slid over her body, moulding her against him until the dark roughness of his body hair rasped against the delicacy of her breasts and a surging thrust of desire made her gasp and melt against him, arching into him, driven mad by a need to be part of him.

'Brooke.' His mouth found the tender cord of her throat and his teeth nipped softly into her skin, sending shivering waves of sensation spreading through her, the rough rasp of his tongue as it stroked along her throat making her ache with need.

'You're beautiful.' He released her, pushing her down into the settee, studying her with sombre intensity, his hand dark against the paleness of her hip, his thumb probing the barrier of her tiny briefs.

As he bent over her Brooke felt her senses swim with delirious anticipation. This was nothing like how she had imagined their lovemaking would be. She had envisaged him as a tender, slightly distant lover making allowances for her inexperience, but instead he seemed to be as unable to control his responses as she was her own and the result was a fierce, explosive need that seemed to grow with every look and touch. She could almost feel the tension in his body; the hunger that fed on hers, and deliberately drew it out as his fingers stroked her skin, upwards over the narrow indentation of her waist, exploring her rib cage, cupping the fullness of her breasts.

Her breath caught in her throat as he bent over her, touching the aching hardness of her nipples with his tongue, teasing them with its lightly moist caresses until the hunger inside her threatened to explode and she reached up, capturing his head with a small moan of need that seemed to need no explanation. His mouth opened warmly over her breast, his teeth grating erotically over the tender skin.

Brooke was barely aware of digging her nails into his back, or of arching fiercely beneath him, or indeed of the effect her feverish response had had on him until she heard the hoarse sound he made as he released one breast to caress the other, his body hard with arousal as it held her against the settee.

The waistband of his trousers was an impediment her shaking fingers didn't want. She wanted to feel all of him against her. She wanted. . . . She gave a smothered cry of pleasure, her frantic movements stilling as she felt the erotic pull of his mouth against her breast, the laboured sound of Adam's breathing mingling with her soft cries of pleasure.

Suddenly she could wait no longer. 'Adam . . . please. . . .' she implored huskily. 'Please. . . .' He shifted his weight a little, his hand going to his belt while she watched in feverish fascination, and then like iced water being poured down her spine the instrusive sound of the telephone broke the spell of their lovemaking. She shivered with cold and shock as Adam moved away from her, turning his back to her as he spoke into the receiver.

'Susan . . . no of course I don't mind. . . .' Brooke heard him say. 'Yes, tomorrow night is fine. . . . No I don't have any other engagements and even if I did. . . .' He laughed, and Brooke crept off the settee clutching her clothes, shame burning a scorching flame over her skin. How could she have been so stupid?

She heard Adam come to her door and knock gently, calling her name, but for her pride's sake she pretended to be asleep. She couldn't bear to face him now. What on earth could she say? How could she explain away her behaviour? It wouldn't

have been so bad if Adam didn't know that she
was still a virgin. Had she been experienced she
could have lied glibly and said her behaviour was
the result of natural frustration; just as his
response to her had been the natural response of a
highly sexed male to the overtures of an available
woman.

She barely slept, waking in time to hear Adam
moving about. She shrank back under the
bedclothes when he knocked and walked into her
room, holding a tray.

'Toast and coffee,' he told her curtly, avoiding
looking at her. 'Brooke. . . .'

'Adam. . . .'

They both spoke together, both breaking off to
look at the other. 'Brooke, you can't stay here any
longer,' Adam told her firmly when she fell silent.
'Neither are you well enough to go back to the
Lodge alone. . . .' He turned away from her
drumming irate fingers against the wall. 'I own a
villa in the South of France. A French couple run
it for me. I normally visit it a couple of times a
year, the rest of the time it's let out to friends . . .
It's empty at the moment, and I've made
arrangements for you to recuperate there. You're
booked on a flight at lunchtime today. Don't
worry about clothes and things. I've spoken to the
LeBruns, all that will be taken care of at their end.
Madame LeBrun will take you shopping. . . .'

'I'm to go there alone?'

She hated herself for asking the question but
was completely unable to resist.

'The LeBruns will be there to take care of you.'
Adam avoided her eyes. 'A month should be long
enough to see you sufficiently recovered.'

'And my job?' Brooke asked him tightly,

knowing the answer, her heart sinking as she waited for it. Adam guessed how she felt about him, and as she had known he would, he didn't want to get involved with her. Adam didn't want love in his life, he wanted a sexually compatible, experienced woman who shared his views on life, not an over-romantic virgin.

'We'll review the position once you're well enough. My existing PA has agreed to stay on for an extra month—her baby isn't due for two, and she's feeling well enough to go on working. . . .'

'Adam. . . .' Hating herself for doing it Brooke reached out towards him, sensing his withdrawal even though he didn't move. Every bone in his face was rigid with tension.

'It's for the best Brooke,' he told her unemotionally. 'I think last night showed us both that, I can't keep you here any longer without taking you to my bed. . . .'

'And?' she asked, her heart in her mouth. Perhaps if she told him she knew the rules and accepted them . . . but her hopes were dashed as he responded curtly, 'And I don't want the complications that would involve, and there are complications—we both know that.'

Meaning that he knew—or guessed—how she felt about him, Brooke thought miserably. What could she say? She could insist on going back to the Lodge, where all she could do was sit and brood, or she could give in gracefully to the arrangements he had made and hope that a month away would help her to gather her mental resources to such an extent that she could control her feelings for him. 'Very well.' She bowed her head in acceptance, not looking up until she knew he had left the room, and biting down hard on her lip to stop the tears falling. Susan must possess ESP because Brooke knew that without her telephone call last night by now she and Adam would have been lovers, and the dreadful thing was that even knowing he didn't love her, she still wanted them to be. Adam was right, it was best that she left, best for her and best for him.

CHAPTER SEVEN

HER flight to Nice was uneventful, and as Brooke stepped off the plane to sombre clouds and light drizzle she felt that the weather was reflecting her moods. She hadn't cried since Adam had made his decision to send her away, but the tears were there clogging up her throat, held back only by a fierce effort of will.

He had driven her to the airport and waited with her for her flight. It had been an agony she hadn't wanted to endure, knowing who he would be spending his evening with. No doubt tonight his physical hunger would be appeased, while she. . . .

Like someone in a trance Brooke passed through Customs barely aware of the covert looks of interest the Customs Officer gave her. In the arrivals hall she found the LeBruns without too much difficulty; a small, dapper French couple they were holding up a cardboard notice with her name on it, and greeted her in careful English when she made herself known to them.

Brooke's own French was good, and she could sense their relief when she switched to that language. It came as something of a shock to learn from them that Adam was fluent in their language, although once she thought about it she could understand how, with his quick grasp of the essentials and hard-headed determination, he would soon pick up enough of any language to get by on. Adam would never trust anyone else to interpret for him; he would always prefer to deal with others direct, whether in a business or any other capacity.

'Monsieur Hart said that we were to take you shopping,' Madame LeBrun informed Brooke as they led her to the car park. 'He said that you did not have time to pack suitable clothes before you left England.'

As she glanced at the sullen sky Brooke grimaced briefly. Her London suit was eminently suitable for such dull weather, but she felt too tired to argue, and it was true that she was getting heartily sick of the couple of changes of clothes she had originally packed for her brief trip to London.

A telephone call to the Dower House before she left for the airport had assured her that Tod and Balsebar were getting along very well. Tod assured her that the dog was no trouble and promised her that he would continue to look after him for her.

'Just get yourself well,' had been his parting words to her, but how did she cure herself of a broken heart, Brooke wondered achingly as they sped through the streets of Nice and then started to head out of the town and up into the hills.

Adam's villa was close to Juan Les Pins and would be, Brooke suspected, quite spectacular. When she had left London people had been busy with their Christmas shopping, and the pain inside her grew as she thought of spending Christmas here, virtually alone. She would have been alone had she remained in England she reminded herself, but there at least her surroundings would have been familiar. Her solicitor's wife would have no doubt invited her over for Christmas lunch, and there had been a tentative invitation from Jeff Gibson to go with him to the local Hunt Ball.

How would Adam spend the Christmas holiday? Ski-ing in Gstaad or somewhere similar, with Susan? A jagged fork of pain tore at her heart and she turned her head towards the window, hoping that Madame LeBrun who was sitting in the back of the car with her, wouldn't notice her momentary weakness. She had spent several holidays in Switzerland in her teens, and thoroughly enjoyed ski-ing, but it wasn't *that* that she envied Susan, it was Adam's presence; his lovemaking; his. . . .

'Soon we will be there,' Madame LeBrun told her, interrupting her unhappy thoughts. They had driven through the village and turned off down a narrow lane that seemed to meander past high walls and concealing hedges. When at last they turned into a gravelled drive, Brooke tried to take an interest in her surroundings, apathy quickly changing to genuine interest as she realised that she had been wrong in assuming that Adam would own a modern, showy villa. The building she could see emerging at the end of the drive was old and creeper clad, hugging the contours of the land. Beneath the creeper the walls glowed a soft, warm cream, and as the car stopped outside the main door Brooke was conscious of an almost physical aura of peace.

'How lovely it is.' She barely whispered the words, climbing out of the car to study her surroundings.

'Many years ago this land was owned by the monks,' Madame LeBrun told her. 'It was here in Monsieur Hart's house that they once made their remedies from the herbs that grow locally.'

Almost reverently Brooke touched the mellow stone. Had it been its association with the monks

that had persuaded Adam to buy Abbot's
Meade? Who, owning this villa, could not help
but be impressed by the soothing air of peace its
original owners had left behind them? Abbot's
Meade had it too, she recognised, but to a much
lesser extent.

'Come. . . .' Madame LeBrun touched her arm,
smiling understandingly as though she knew how
deeply the villa affected her. The main doors
opened on to a tiled hallway, decorated in soft
cream and rich terracotta. Several doors opened
off it and Madame LeBrun opened one indicating
that Brooke precede her. She found herself in an
elegant and yet welcoming salon, furnished simply
in the same rich creams and terracotta as the hall,
only with the addition of pure jades and blues,
colours which would reflect those of the sea and
the sky in midsummer, Brooke realised.

Beyond the elegant French windows lay the
gardens; mostly formal flower beds, framed by
hedges. 'The pool and tennis courts lie beyond the
hedge,' Madame LeBrun explained to her. 'The
pool is empty at the moment, but if you would
care to use it. . . .'

Quickly Brooke shook her head, feeling the
effects of her journey.

'You are tired,' Madame LeBrun sympathised
'I shall show you to your room and tomorrow we
shall attack the shops.' When Brooke would have
objected she said firmly, 'Monsieur Hart has given
me my instructions.' Her face softened into a
smile. 'If you will come this way.'

The stairs were narrow and twisty, leading up to
a rectangular gallery. Four doors led off it.

'As you can see the villa is not large. It has but
four bedrooms.' Madame LeBrun explained

adding, 'Monsieur LeBrun and myself have an apartment over the garages.'

She opened one of the doors and gestured Brooke inside. The room was a pleasant size, overlooking a small cobbled courtyard, complete with a dovecot. Brooke felt her breath catch, an almost unbearable mingling of pain and nostalgia sweeping over her. As if she closed her eyes and listened to the doves she might almost be able to believe she was back at Abbot's Meade.

'You do not care for the room?' Madame LeBrun sounded concerned. 'But Monsieur Hart told me to give you this one most particularly.'

'I love the room,' Brooke assured her in a shaky voice. Her composure was far too fragile for her to endure hearing that Adam had given such specific instructions for her comfort, and it was true, she did love the room. Decorated in pale yellows and peach it seemed to glow with sunlight, despite the overcast sky outside.

It had its own small bathroom, which Madame LeBrun showed her, and when she had left Brooke alone, promising to bring up a soothing tisane which would help her sleep, Brooke sank down into the peach wicker chair by the window and stared unseeingly out into the gardens.

Which room was Adam's? A deep shudder wracked through her body as she remembered the scene in his apartment the previous night. If she closed her eyes it was still possible for her to recreate the scent and feel of his half-naked body; she could even re-live the responses of her own to him, but nothing could bring the reality of Adam into this room with her, no matter how much she longed for him.

She was glad when Madame LeBrun arrived

with the tisane because it broke the powerful spell
of her thoughts.

As the Frenchwoman had prophesied it helped
her to sleep, but as she lay, drifting aimlessly in the
half world between waking and sleeping, all
Brooke's thoughts were concentrated on Adam.
Was he with Susan now? Was he holding her,
making love to her as he had made love to *her* last
night? No, not as he had made love to *her*, Brooke
thought with fierce anguish, with Susan in his
arms he would know no hesitation; no fear of
commitment. . . .

Was that why he had held off with her, Brooke
wondered bitterly, because despite all he had said
about not wanting any involvement, in his heart of
hearts he was still the young boy she had rejected,
the young boy who still yearned hopelessly for the
princess he had put on an ivory pedestal? Well, if
he had Susan was more than ready to step down
off that pedestal, Brooke thought miserably; and
very much more than ready to show Adam that
she was all too human. Adam was a rich man now
and Susan was a divorced woman looking for a
second husband wealthy enough to support her in
comfort. Her thoughts jumbling painfully, Brooke
at last fell asleep.

'We will drive into Cannes for there are to be
found the best shops,' Madame LeBrun pronounced. She was in Brooke's room watching with
an eagle eye while Brooke bit into a rich, flaky
croissant, coated with delicious apricot preserve. A
large cup of fragrant French coffee waited at her
elbow. This was spoiling indeed Brooke thought
lethargically. Breakfast in bed. Unwanted an image
of Adam bringing her toast and coffee on her last

morning in his apartment rose up before her, and suddenly she wanted to cry.

Suppressing her emotions she tried to concentrate on what Madame LeBrun was saying. The Frenchwoman dressed very elegantly and today she was wearing a neat navy dress that Brooke suspected cost far more than she would ever dream of spending on one outfit. She wanted to protest that she didn't need any clothes, but knew that she would be lying. Even so, she hated the thought of spending Adam's money. She had a little of her own saved, and the minute she returned to England she would make a point of reimbursing him for every penny that she spent.

Madame LeBrun was a competent driver, parking the Renault carefully in a specially designated area, not far from the shopping arcades.

As she followed her through the crowded streets, Brooke was swept by a painful surge of homesickness as she watched the busy shoppers laden with Christmas presents.

'I am afraid that we shall be away from the house on Christmas Day,' Madame LeBrun apologised to Brooke. 'My father who is very old already expects us, otherwise. . . .'

'No, please . . . of course you must not even think of changing your arrangements for me.' Brooke assured her quickly. What would Adam be doing on Christmas Day? Lunching with Susan and her parents, no longer a young upstart, but a wealthy businessman whose achievements made him an accepted member of their family circle? How could Adam be taken in by her, Brooke wondered achingly; Susan might be beautiful, but she was also hard; and Brooke doubted that she cared any more for the real Adam; the man he was inside the image he had built for himself, than she had cared for Adam the boy. No, what Susan wanted was the outer Adam; the wealthy, assured, predatory male he had become.

Reminding herself that all she was doing was making the pain worse for herself Brooke tried to concentrate as Madame LeBrun led her from boutique to boutique. At last, obviously at a loss to understand her lack of interest, the Frenchwoman's eyes brightened. 'I know just the place,' she informed Brooke. 'A countrywoman of yours who has married a Frenchman; she owns a small boutique just down here.'

'Down here' was a narrow, but charming alleyway occupied by several discreetly fronted and obviously expensive shops. Madame LeBrun paused outside one of them and then went in.

The woman who stepped forward to serve them glanced thoughtfully at Brooke as Madame LeBrun explained in voluble French what was required.

'Please,' Brooke interrupted, visions of her small bank balance diminishing far too rapidly hovering unpleasantly before her eyes, 'I'm not really looking for anything special, just something to tide me over for a few weeks.'

'That is a pity, all clothes should be special,' the other woman smiled. 'Indeed I like to think that all *my* clothes *are* special. You are here for a month you say. . . . That will include the Christmas period. . . . You will surely need something special for that . . . unless of course you have already brought something with you?'

Unwilling to admit that she would be spending Christmas Day completely alone Brooke allowed herself to be seated on a surprisingly comfortable cane chair while cupboards were opened and clothes produced.

'This I think would become you admirably. . . .' Lovingly the proprietress displayed a tawny velvet outfit for Brooke's inspection. A skirt and top, the skirt was pencil shaped and very elegant. The top was the same rich colour as the skirt but in a heavy satin, the full sleeves caught up in velvet cuffs. The waist also was banded in velvet the top flouncing out into a flattering peplum, but it was the back of the top that caught Brooke's attention. Geometrically shaped into a squared off 'U' it fastened at the waist with three small velvet covered buttons.

The moment she touched the deep velvet pile Brooke knew she had to have the outfit no matter how expensive it was. Deriding herself for her folly she allowed herself to be persuaded into it. As she had known instinctively it would, it fitted her perfectly. Even Madame LeBrun gasped in appreciative approval when she stepped out of the changing cubicle to examine her reflection properly in the floor-length mirrors.

'C'est magnifique,' she pronounced. 'That colour is so right for you. . . .'

As she turned round Brooke caught a glimpse of her back; the curve of her spine surprisingly vulnerable, her skin a gleaming, almost pearlescent cream against the dark tawny fabric.

'It is perfect for you,' the proprietress told her truthfully, 'and if you should need underwear—'

The silk satin camisole she produced had the same cutaway back. Plainly, almost severely tailored the fabric clung sensuously to Brooke's fingers, completely free of lace, the garment's only adornment was the delicately appliqued butterflies

adorning both the low back and moulding the top
of the beautifully shaped cups.

A suspender belt to match was produced and
some toning silk stockings, and Brooke knew that
she was lost. She simply had to have them all, if
only for the anguish of wishing Adam could see
her wearing them. Intuitively she knew that Adam
would approve of her choice and that he would far
rather she spent all her money on one undeniably
feminine outfit than on half-a-dozen more practical
ones.

She would never go anywhere this Christmas
where she could wear such a luxurious outfit,
Brooke thought despairingly as she paid for her
purchases, and yet the feminine side of her nature
couldn't regret them.

'Now shoes,' Madame LeBrun announced
firmly when they had left the shop 'and then for
everyday wear Les Tweeds. . . .'

Shoes weren't hard to find. Madame LeBrun
knew a small sidestreet shop that specialised in
cut-price Dior models and Brooke, with her long
narrow feet, had no problem in finding a pair of
softly supple suede shoes which exactly matched
her outfit.

Madame LeBrun's idea of 'Les Tweeds' turned
out to be a range of softly toning pastel tweed
skirts and silk shirts and cashmere jumpers, and
suspecting that she would bitterly regret it later
Brooke allowed herself to be tempted into an
incredibly soft tweed skirt in muted oatmeals
with a toning russet silk blouse and a matching
oatmeal cashmere sweater.

To appease her feelings of guilt Brooke also
bought herself a pair of jeans and several
cheerful tops to wear about the villa. After all

she was supposed to be recuperating, not socialising.

On their way back to Juan Les Pins Madame LeBrun explained that the area was very quiet during the holiday season, very few visitors arriving. 'Les Alps or cruising, that is what they prefer these days,' she told Brooke with a smile.

It was a full week before Brooke stopped expecting to hear from Adam, but nothing could stop her imagination from tormenting her with pictures of him—both alone and with Susan.

Madame LeBrun had told her that she was to make herself completely at home in the villa, but Brooke had been reluctant to do more than make the odd brief telephone call to Abbot's Meade to check on Balsebar.

On both occasions she spoke to Tod, who told her that her dog was fine. 'Adam takes him for his walks when he's down here, but he's been spending a lot of time in London.'

Tod hadn't said any more, but Brooke had guessed who Adam's time had been spent with.

The weather changed, and became mild and balmy. Brooke felt well enough to wander down to the small pebbly beach the villa shared with several others on the small peninsula. As she had anticipated it was deserted, but she had enjoyed the clean fresh breeze coming off the water, huddled warmly inside the thick camel coat she had brought with her from London.

She had written to her few friends in England, telling them where she was, and had a very anxious letter back from the Brockbanks.

As Brooke had expected the couple had intended to invite her over for Christmas lunch and she sighed as she put the letter on one side. She was going to be lonely, but she had tried to keep such thoughts at bay. She couldn't expect the LeBruns to change their plans merely on her account and Adam had doubtless not given a thought to Christmas when he had sent her away. She wondered about changing her flight and going home a week early, but the flight was already booked and she felt reluctant to change it in case Adam thought she was chasing him.

As the days slid by Brooke knew that she was gradually recovering from her illness. She felt fitter, healthier, but underlying the soft glow colouring her skin, was a tension that had nothing to do with her illness. Despite Madame LeBrun's appetising meals she hadn't put on any weight, and knew that she was a little too thin. She could feel her ribs, and her hip bones projected noticeably. Even her face had a fine-drawn, fragile delicacy, and although the doctor Adam had instructed to call weekly and check up on her frowned over her weight he had to admit that in other quarters her health gave no concern at all.

He was a plump, balding man with a harassed smile and warm brown eyes, and when he learned that Brooke was spending Christmas on her own, he had frowned, tapping his fingers against the door of her room while he considered the matter.

'I am a widower,' he said at last, 'and because I have no family I normally spend Christmas Day in the children's ward of our local hospital—this enables the other doctors to have time off to be with their families. If you would care for it, I should be able to arrange for you to join us—for the sake of the children we try to make their Christmas as joyful as possible—we have several

long-stay patients who for one reason or another
have no one of their own who can be with them on
Christmas Day, and visitors are always much
appreciated by them.'

When Brooke realised that his invitation was
quite genuine, she felt her spirits lift a little. Where
better to lose her melancholy longings for Adam
than in the busy bustle of the hospital?

'I accept, but only on condition that I'm allowed
to make myself useful,' she told Doctor Beunne.

'Oh you will do that all right,' he promised her.
'The children are always willing to be read to, or
otherwise entertained.'

After that Brooke found it easier to face the
prospect of Christmas. Her cards had been bought
and sent off several days before the doctor's visit,
but now she borrowed the Renault and drove
herself into Cannes, raiding the stores for suitable
presents for the children. On Christmas Eve she
waved the LeBruns off in their own small car with
a lighter heart than she could have thought
possible a week before, her only indulgence being
the half hour or so she spent dreaming of Adam as
she sat in front of a log fire in the main salon, and
wondered what he was doing, and whether he had
given any thought to her.

Hardly likely, she mocked herself, remembering
that he hadn't even sent her a card, or telephoned
her. When she did go home would her job still be
open, or would he find some excuse to get rid of
her? Sighing faintly she stared into the fire,
wishing the patterns they made did not always
somehow resemble Adam's profile.

On Christmas morning she woke up early. For
once there was none of the familiarly childish
anticipation that there might have been snow

during the night. She showered quickly, dressing in her new tawny velvet. Not just for her sake but for the children's as well she told herself as she went downstairs and breakfasted off croissants and preserve.

Enough food to withstand a seige filled the huge refrigerator, and tonight when she returned from the hospital she fully intended to make herself a traditional meal, using the turkey Madame LeBrun had cooked especially for her.

In one corner of the salon stood the small artificial tree she had bought in Cannes, glittering with the decorations she had put on it. Turning swiftly away Brooke tried not to think of other Christmases when her parents and her uncle had been alive, family Christmases full of laughter and warmth. Nor was she going to allow herself to dwell on the sort of Christmas that would fulfil every one of her dearest held dreams; Adam and herself before a roaring fire in the Dower House drawing room, a huge tree glimmering in one corner, while a couple of toddlers played energetically with Santa's munificence.

Driving the Renault she arrived at the hospital in good time, having experienced no problem in locating it.

By the time she had parked the car and extricated herself and her brightly wrapped presents from inside it Doctor Beunne was waiting for her.

The hospital was only a small one, specialising mainly in children's cases, he explained as he led the way down a gleaming corridor, Mingling with all the normal hospital smells were others ... fragrant and tantalising ... the eternal smells of Christmas, good food, excitement ... pine needles. . . .

'We do cater for mainly private patients, but the profit we make on that side of things allows us to operate this ward for those who are not as financially well off.' He paused as he spoke to push open a heavy door, and Brooke grinned at the scene she saw as she stepped inside.

The ward had been decorated especially for the occasion, and with true French élan. No drooping streamers here, no tired balloons or tarnished tinsel. . . . Instead the walls of the ward had been painted with brilliant Christmassy scenes, one end of it dominated by a huge Christmas tree, laden down with decorations. A cheerful nurse was pushing a trolley from bed to bed, handing out glasses of fruit juice to those well enough to drink, and the level of noise was unbelievable.

Children of all ages and in varying stages of recuperation were stripping wrapping paper from gifts, and as Brooke saw one small child manfully struggling with a huge parcel and two heavy plaster casts she felt betraying tears prick her eyes.

'The children are unbelievable,' Dr Beunne whispered to her. 'They throw themselves whole-heartedly into the festivities, even the sickest of them, and I'm afraid that many of them in here are extremely fragile.

'At this hospial we specialise in diseases of the bone,' he added in explanation. 'In some cases we make good progress—almost miraculous progress, but in others. . . .' His expressive shrug said what could not be put into words, and forcing down her pity Brooke followed him to the first bed.

Four hours later, exhausted but feeling more at peace with herself than she had done in months, she left the hospital, driving the Renault back to the villa. She had read until she was hoarse; had played a variety of silly games, eaten far too much food, laughed until she had cried and sometimes just cried for the sheer bravery of the children she was watching. Now she felt drained both emotionally and physically, but she would not have missed the experience for anything. . . . Not even to sit and daydream over Adam, she told herself bleakly.

Dusk started to fall as she reached the villa. She parked the Renault and let herself in, telling herself firmly that she wasn't going to brood. No one in good health had any right to do that after what she had seen today.

After setting a match to the logs in the salon she went into the kitchen, still wearing her finery, and started to prepare the evening meal she no longer really wanted. But Madame LeBrun would be upset if she ate nothing, after all her careful preparations. It seemed silly to eat in solitary splendour in the attractive dining room with its delicate reproduction furniture and silk-panelled walls, but nevertheless that was what she was going to do.

An hour later, having renewed her make-up and brushed her hair Brooke was just on the way to check on her dinner when the doorbell chimed.

Her initial thought was that someone had come to the wrong house, followed by a quick stab of anxiety. . . . What if someone knew she was here alone. . . .? The villa was expensively furnished with many fine antiques. Trying to dispel her nervousness she opened the door, keeping it on the safety catch. It was too dark outside for her to make out the features of the man standing there, but his voice was instantly familiar, and Brooke felt a wave of disbelief storm through her as Adam said, drawling mockingly, 'I hope I'm not too late for dinner. What we were offered on the plane was like sawdust. . . .'

As she unhooked the safety chain with trembling fingers and stood back to let him in Brooke tried to gather together her disordered thoughts. Once he was inside she could see that Adam looked tired and drawn, his cheek bones harshly prominent, his eyes glittering with the intensity she remembered so well.

'Adam, I wasn't expecting you.'

How trite her words sounded, and as he stood still and studied her Brooke felt the deep hectic rhythm of her pulses and the uneven thudding of her heart.

'No. . . .' His look was searching, almost brooding as it slid over her satin and velvet outfit. 'But obviously you were expecting someone.'

'I was out earlier—visiting a children's hospital—Dr Beunne knew I'd be on my own and invited me there. I got dressed up for the children. . . .' Unknowingly her chin lifted, her eyes defying him to guess that she had dressed up, aching with the knowledge that he would never see her in her finery.

'I hope they appreciated it—them and Dr Beunne.' His voice taunted and grated over delicate nerves, rasping against them until Brooke quivered in mute response.

'I'm hungry,' Adam announced briefly. 'I'll go up and shower, we'll have dinner and then we'll talk.'

'Talk?' Alarm feathered along Brooke's veins. What had he come to talk about? Had he come to tell her that he didn't want her working for him?

But why on Christmas Day? And where was Susan?

'Yes. You don't have any objection to talking to me, do you?' he asked sardonically. 'Contrary to what you give every appearance of believing, my little virgin, talk on its own is not sufficient to accomplish a seduction.'

As he moved past her Brooke caught the faintly sweet scent of alcohol on his breath. Had he been drinking? Was that the reason for his strangely cryptic remarks?

'How long will dinner be?'

'Half an hour.' She swallowed tensely, wondering if she was actually participating in this bizzarre exchange or if she had somehow strayed into an illusory world.

'Fine, I'll be down in twenty minutes.'

Adam was gone while she was still pinching herself. She flinched from the small pain. It was real enough all right. Adam was here.

CHAPTER EIGHT

WHEN he reappeared Adam had changed out of his cords and sweater into a dinner suit.

'It seemed appropriate in view of your own finery,' he told her, deftly uncorking the bottle of red wine she had decided to drink with her meal. 'Children's hospitals seem to find favour with you. I remember you donoted most of the surplus cash from the sale of Abbot's Meade to one.'

'We all have out little foibles,' Brooke retorted smoothly. 'Yours seems to be a prediliction for old monasteries.'

'At least for the buildings, if not the lifestyle, you mean,' Adam mocked, shrugging lightly as he said, 'In both instances it was the air of peace that attracted me, I can't deny that, but that's as far as my "prediliction" as you call it goes.'

He followed Brooke into the kitchen and started carving the turkey while she removed dishes from the oven.

'Traditional Christmas fare,' he commented, pausing to watch her. 'Planning to eat all alone were you?'

'As this isn't my home I'm hardly likely to invite other people into it,' Brooke responded grimly. She was getting tired of the cat and mouse game Adam seemed to be playing with her. There was a finely drawn tension about him she couldn't understand. It was almost as though in some way he resented her.

'Why did you come here Adam?' she asked him when they were sitting down, eating.

'I already told you, I want to talk to you.'

'On Christmas Day? Somehow I envisaged you having far too much to do to think about me.'

'Meaning?'

Shrugging lightly Brooke told him. 'I anticipated that you would probably be spending the day with Susan and her parents.'

'Did you indeed. That was a pretty spectacular piece of mental arithmetic, wasn't it. As a matter of fact I *was* invited but I refused.'

Hope, sharp and heady as champagne bubbles rose giddily inside her, her nerves tingling in nervous response as Adam suddenly pushed his plate away and stood up coming round to her side of the table.

When his hands went to her shoulders, drawing her up out of her seat she followed their commands unresistingly. 'Brooke, I've flown God knows how many miles to be with you today, and it wasn't just so that I could eat Christmas Dinner with you.'

'Then what was it for,' Brooke heard herself ask, her voice an unrecognisable, provocative whisper, her body already melting towards Adam's.

'This.'

Fiercely exultant joy swept tumultuously through her as Adam bent his head and kissed her savagely, the tension she had sensed in him before increasing as she felt the strain of his muscles compacting beneath the hands she slid up under his jacket. His heart thudded unevenly against her palm, his tongue prising her lips apart, subtlety abandoned as he shook with the hunger she could feel building up inside him.

Strangely she felt neither resentment nor fear,

only a leaping, excited response that enabled her to meet and match the intensity of his possessive kiss, giving herself up to it, and glorying in the fierce heat that raged through them both.

When at last he lifted his head Adam's breathing was ragged. He hadn't made any move to touch her in any other way, but Brooke knew now irrevocably that they would make love and the tiny ache in the pit of her stomach grew, and clamoured for appeasement.

'You wanted that as much as I did.' It was a statement rather than a question, and Brooke held his gaze as Adam stared at her. 'You want me to make love to you,' he persisted thickly. 'You know you do Brooke.'

'Have I denied it?' Her quiet tone seemed to shock him. The grey eyes dilated and glittered brilliantly. 'You were the one who sent me away, Adam.'

'Because I didn't. . . . Oh hell, why are we wasting time talking,' he muttered rawly reaching for her, his hands moulding her along the length of his body, letting her feel the extent of his need and hunger for her.

'I want to take you to bed and make love to you in all the ways I've dreamed of making love to you from the first moment I saw you.'

The passionate words shivered across her skin, and misinterpreting the reason for her light tremor, Adam told her hoarsely, 'Don't be afraid, I shan't hurt you . . . God, Brooke. . . .'

'I want you.' 'And I love you,' she whispered soundlessly, as the words were torn from her aching throat. Her love was a secret she must keep to herself and not burden Adam with. By some miracle he was here with her now where she had dreamed of him being; wanting her almost it seemed to the point of madness, and she was going to take what he offered and treasure it for all time.

'Then come to me now.'

They went upstairs together hand in hand and Brooke knew that he was deliberately giving her time to change her mind. Outside the bedroom door which she now knew was his he paused, his hands resting lightly on her shoulders, his eyes sombre as he studied her. 'This is your last chance to back out Brooke,' he told her thickly. 'Come with me now and I shan't stop until I've made you completely mine.'

'And I shan't want you to,' Brooke whispered back, deliberately pushing open the door and walking into the room.

It was furnished in masculine creams and plums. She had been in it only once before, one morning when she had been looking for Madame LeBrun and on that occasion she hadn't lingered, finding the thought of doing so, of imagining Adam lying in the vastness of the large bed, probably not alone, too much to tolerate. Now although she quivered with tension there was no thought in her mind other than that Adam would be her lover. Her first lover and possibly her only lover she thought achingly, watching him with eyes unknowingly dark gold.

'You're trembling.' Adam reached out, his fingertips touching the smooth skin of her face, tracing along her cheek bone and down to her jaw before he lightly caressed the mobile outline of her mouth.

'Don't be afraid.'

'I'm not.' Her voice trembled too, but not from fear; no, her tremors came from love; from desire

and need, and a fiercely exultant excitement,
Brooke thought achingly, closing her eyes and
allowing her other senses to feast themselves on
Adam's nearness.

She felt his hands on her shoulders, caressing
the narrow bones, smoothing the silk of her top
over them and quivers of pulsing excitement
darted over her skin. She reached for him,
automatically sliding her palms beneath the
thickness of his jacket and round his back, feeling
the tension gripping his muscles as she touched
him.

'Brooke.' He kissed her lightly, muttering her
name in an oddly thick voice, and then kissed her
again, one hand cupping her jaw while the fingers
of the other tangled in her hair, his control
abandoned as he felt her passionate response. This
was what she wanted; this fierce, hungry passion
that overwhelmed every other more rational
emotion; this aching need to be part of another
human being; this blazing, exultant pleasure in
knowing that Adam wanted her with the same
intensity. Her hands left his back to clasp the back
of his head, her fingers weaving insistently in the
thick darkness of his hair. While he was kissing
her Adam had unfastened the three buttons
securing her top and now he moved her lightly
away from him so that he could ease her out of it
completely. His fingers were deft on the zip of her
skirt, his movements economical and yet subtly
caressing so that she felt no embarrassment or
reserve, merely an eager desire to be rid of the
trappings of civilisation, to have as her only
covering the hard warmth of his body.

'This is delicious,' he murmured against her
skin, touching his mouth lightly to the valley

between her breasts as he eased the straps of her
camisole down over her arms, 'but it doesn't feel
as silkily enticing as your skin. Undress me
Brooke,' he commanded thickly, lifting his head to
watch her through narrowed eyelids. How could
she ever have thought his eyes cold? Now they
glowed like molten metal, blazing with the same
need she could feel twisting and turning in her own
body. 'You can't know how much I've burned to
feel your hands against my skin ... ached for it,'
he muttered unsteadily as her fingers moved
tentatively to the buttons on his shirt.

To help her he shed his jacket, shrugging it on
to the floor, his lips teasing light kisses along the
side of her throat and down on to her shoulder.

'You're trembling,' he told her softly as she
struggled with the second button.

'How can you expect me to concentrate on what
I'm doing,' Brooke protested in response, 'when
you keep on kissing me like that?'

She felt the warmth of his laughter graze her
skin, and instead of feeling gauche she felt a spurt
of warm pleasure, knowing that his laughter had
been indulgent rather than mocking.

'I can see I'm going to have to teach you how to
do more than one thing at once.' He lifted his
head, and looked at her lazily, as her nervous
fingers stilled.

'There's nothing to stop you kissing me back,'
he told her softly, the heat of his gaze belying the
mildness of his voice, and the fingers he spread
against the back of her head propelled her gently
towards him, until her lips touched the pulse
thudding in his throat.

His skin tasted warm, faintly salty and in some
indefinable way intensely male. The feel of it

beneath her mouth made Brooke grow bolder, and to her amazement the buttons that had proved so irksome suddenly seemed to free themselves from their holes. Dazed by the unexpectedness of the sheer sensual pleasure touching Adam gave her, Brooke lifted her head to find him smiling down at her, the reason for the ease with which the buttons had slid free explained as she saw his fingers entwined with hers.

'Practice makes perfect—in all things,' he told her, gently mocking her, and then as though he understood the pain that rose inside her as she remembered how many women he must have gained his practice with, he added huskily, 'but perfection isn't everything—far from it, it can be a cold, empty thing, without the reality of emotion to warm it.'

Emotion? What was he saying? That he cared for her? No, if that was the case Adam would have come right out and said so. Could he have guessed how she felt about him? For a moment Brooke felt almost dizzy with shock and despair, but then she conquered her feelings, telling herself fiercely that nothing mattered except that Adam was here and that he had flown to France especially to be with her. Could the way she felt about him, the need she felt to express that love in all the ways she could, cancel out her lack of physical experience? She would make it, she decided fiercely; she would make memories tonight that would stay not just with her for all her life but with him as well.

That decision once made dissolved her last few remaining inhibitions. Her fingertips investigated the narrow opening of tanned skin, roughened by fine dark hairs, exposed by the open shirt buttons, her lips once again tasting the smooth skin of

Adam's throat. His muscles tensed and hardened
beneath her touch, the low groan her explorative
touch brought ripping from his taut throat inciting
her to tease his warm skin with the tip of her
tongue, trailing it along the strong column of his
throat as he arched it in hungry supplication of her
touch, muttering her name hoarsely as he cupped
the warm firmness of her breasts with hands that
trembled faintly as they touched her skin.

When his thumbs teased the swollen crests of
her breasts Brooke felt her blood heat to molten
wildness, her soft cry of pleasure smothered
against his skin. His teeth nipped delicately at her
earlobe, his tongue stroking quivering paths of fire
along its delicate convolutions.

Almost without her being aware of it Brooke
grasped his shoulders, curling her fingers into his
skin as she mutely begged for an appeasement of
the need his stroking caresses were arousing,
arching her body against his, fiercely pleased by
his hoarse sound of frustration, as his hands slid to
her hips, pressing her against the straining muscles
of his thighs.

'I want to make love to you slowly and
lingeringly,' he muttered rawly into her skin, 'but
if you go on tormenting me like this, we won't
even make it as far as the bed.'

His thickly rasped words heated her skin,
making it ache for the close contact he spoke of.
Tentatively Brooke touched his belt, and felt him
tense. 'Yes, yes, Brooke, touch me.' The fiercely
groaned demand stopped her from withdrawing,
giving her the confidence to unfasten the buckle
and reach hesitantly for his zip.

The shudder that ripped through him beneath
her light touch inflamed her own responses.

Suddenly she felt as provocative and irresistible as the most experienced seductress. Her body thrilled to the knowledge that she could make him feel like this; that she could make him ache and hunger for her in the same way that she ached and hungered for him.

'Stop.'

His harshly whispered command shattered her self-confidence, scattering it in a million tiny fragments. Tense and shivering she stared up at him, not knowing what she had done wrong, or why his face should look so tense and strained.

'Dear God Brooke, don't look at me like that.' His voice was a thread of sound, huskily punctuating the heavy silence of his bedroom. His hands framed her face, his thumbs stroking soothingly over her heated skin.

'I want you so badly, you're making me shake like an adolescent. If only you weren't so damned innocent.' She barely heard his last comment, because his face was buried against her skin, but she could feel the tension emanating from him; the perspiration beading his forehead, just as she could sense the relentless urgency building up inside him. For a moment she felt vulnerable and bitterly angry that she could not meet him on his own terms; that she lacked the experience that he seemed to wish she had, but then her love for him surged through her, overpowering every negative reaction. Somehow, despite her lack of experience, she would make him forget his reservations.

'Once you told me you liked it,' she reminded him bravely.

'Once I believed I had the self-control to cope with it,' he responded dryly, 'but then I wasn't holding you in my arms with my hunger for you threatening to get way, way out of control.' There was a hint of bitter savagery beneath the self-mockery in his voice that both thrilled and scared her.

'I want you Adam,' she said at last, overcoming her nervous qualms, and looking straight at him. 'I'm sorry if my lack of experience puts you off. . . .'

'Puts me off!' He groaned huskily, obviously torn between laughter and impatience. 'Oh Brooke, you don't even begin to understand. . . .'

'I understand that my body aches for yours,' she told him softly, holding his gaze. 'I understand that I want you to touch me, to caress me, and that I want to do the same to you.' She moved slightly and the light from the uncurtained window fell across her body, outlining the curved purity of her breasts. Adam made a sound deep in his throat so primaeval that she shivered as she heard it, watching in a dream as he wrenched off the remainder of his clothes, watching her all the time with a fierce intensity that seemed to hold her in thrall.

His body was every bit as magnificent as she had imagined. Her breath caught faintly in her throat as she stared wide-eyed at him, and then his hands were on her waist, lifting her and carrying her towards the bed.

It dipped under their combined weight and as Brooke's hands came in contact with Adam's chest, she could feel the heat coming off his body. The control and tension she had sensed warring in him both exploded and disintegrated as his hands shaped the outline of her body, and she felt the fierce almost savage surge of need thrust through him, communicated to her by the ferocious urgency of his hands.

It seemed to kindle something deep inside her, something elemental and deep-rooted, so that she became completely malleable and responsive to his touch, almost as though she had been formed with this one purpose in mind.

Freed of the restrictions of habit and self-consciousness Brooke explored Adam's body with a pleasure she had never envisioned herself experiencing. His skin felt hot beneath her touch, his muscles firm against the long bones, his body hardened and toughened so that it felt alien to her fingertips, different from her own familiar softly curving femininity. Suddenly despite Adam's comments she was glad that she had waited for this first time with him; glad that there were no memories or prejudices left over from other lovers to mar the purity of what she was experiencing now. Nothing blurred the intense joy she felt in knowing him, her lips worshipping where her fingers explored, her concentration broken only when she felt Adam shudder and rasp her name thickly, his hands cupping her breasts as they had done earlier, his thumbs rhythmically caressing their hard crests. When his tongue touched them, lightly at first, painting delicate circles round the tender skin, a wild skein of pleasure seemed to tighten convulsively inside her. Her body tensed and then arched, her head thrown back as her hands held the back of his head. Her response seemed to unleash something elemental in Adam, his mouth possessively demanding as it fastened round first one nipple and then the other.

Starbursts of pleasure exploded inside her as Brooke abandoned herself completely to the erotic demands of his mouth. Shivers of pleasure rippled down her spine as she felt the fine grate of his teeth against her tender skin. Her own lips found the column of his throat and the strong curve of his shoulder, her fingers leaving his head to spread possessively against his back.

Adam's hands curled on to her hips, stroking the slender bones, before exploring the rounded shape of her bottom, holding her against the heat of his body.

His mouth left the aching tenderness of her breasts to taste the smooth skin of her throat, upwards along her jaw line, the rough rasp of his body hair against the pleasurably tender flesh of her nipples making her arch and move convulsively against him.

His fingers tightened round her buttocks, and Brooke caught her breath in fierce pleasure as she felt the heated, rhythmic response of his body.

Stroking fingers slid up her spine and tangled in her hair, pulling her head backwards, her small instinctive protest lost beneath the fierce onslaught of a kiss that made her ache and tremble with need.

'Not yet ... not yet,' Adam muttered unsteadily against her swollen mouth as he felt her instinctive and untutored attempt to satisfy her need. His hands moved a little less fiercely over her body as he pushed her slightly away from him, his fingers fanning out possessively across the slight swell of her stomach.

An aching coil of tension twisted deep inside her, and she reached out blindly, pressing her lips to the flat hardness of Adam's nipple, running trembling fingers along the dark line of hair that arrowed down over his flat stomach.

His fiercely convulsive movement betrayed his response, one hand trapping her fingers, the other grasping her chin and tilting it upwards until his tongue could trace the moist warmth of her lips, teasing them until they parted in a soundless moan of pleasure, leaving his tongue free to explore the sweetness of her mouth in a kiss that made her mindless with aching pleasure while his fingers urged hers against his skin, inciting her to an intimate exploration of his male body that brought a throaty purr of satisfaction to his lips and quivers of shivering excitement to her body.

It seemed ridiculous that she had reached the grand old age of twenty-six without knowing the intimacy of a man's body before but now she knew Adam's, and hesitancy gave way to desire and love as she pulled her mouth from his and caressed the moist warmth of his skin with a delicate precision that absorbed her so absolutely that it took Adam's fingers manacled to her wrists to pull her back into his arms.

'Have you any idea what you do to me when you touch me like that?' He muttered the words thickly into her ear, the sound of them interspersed with the heavy, erratic thud of his heart.

'A little,' Brooke responded demurely, self-satisfaction giving way to tumultuous desire as Adam's fingers stroked tantalisingly along her thighs and then between them. He watched the dawn of startled realisation darken her eyes to gold and then give way to an almost unbearable pleasure as she ceased trying to push him away and instead, cried out his name in aching surprise, overwhelmed by the sensations he was arousing.

'That's what you do to me when you touch and kiss me the way you were doing,' he told her rawly. 'You make me ache Brooke, way, way down into my bones and guts.'

'You make me ache too,' Brooke responded huskily far beyond any attempt at dissimulation, and as though her tremulous admission broke down the last barriers of his self-control Adam bent his head, touching his lips to the delicate satiny skin of her waist, the pressure of his mouth growing more and more compulsive as he absorbed the taste and texture of her.

Helplessly out of control Brooke responded feverishly to every command of his mouth and lips, the long awaited weight of his body as it lay between the cradle of her thighs momentarily soothing the deep-seated ache that hungered inside her.

His fingertips stroking up over her skin Adam kissed her closed eyelids. Where it had been feverishly heated his touch was now tender and restrained, but Brooke sensed that it was a finely held restraint, ready to shatter explosively at any second and held on to only for her sake.

Her heart cried out impatiently that it didn't want his restraint and she moved eagerly, urgently, beneath him twining her arms round his neck and lifting her body enticingly to meet his. 'I want you Adam.' She said the words fiercely against his skin, parting her lips hungrily for his kiss, glorying in the first fierce thrust of his body against hers, and welcoming its invasion of her femininity with an impatience that seemed to overwhelm Adam's restraint.

The pain was nothing like what she had expected; brief and lost beneath an overpowering surge of pleasure, her body instinctively matching the urgent rhythm of Adam's, her every sense lost in it until it seemed to time the beat of her heart and the rate of her pulse.

It was a rhythm as elemental as the sea against the shore; as time itself, Brooke thought hazily; something that her body had always secretly known and now exulted in.

Pleasure gave way to aching urgency, her nails raking the hard muscles of Adam's back, her fiercely feminine sounds of pleasure lost beneath his mouth as their shared compulsive need mounted, exploding in dizzying waves of pleasure that crashed down over Brooke almost at the same time as she felt Adam tense, and call out her name, long shudders of release wracking his lean body, as he held her possessively against him, the sound of their shared ragged breathing puncturing the silence of the room.

Minutes later, when Brooke tried to pull away, telling herself that in the aftermath of their lovemaking she must not betray the love she had managed to keep silent about during it, Adam's arms tightened round her, refusing to let her go, his body embracing hers, as though they were lovers mentally as well as physically. It made Brooke want to cry, weak tears filling her eyes and sliding down her face. One dropped on to Adam's skin and he tensed, his tongue touching the salty dampness of her face. Almost before her tears had dried she was falling asleep, her body pleasantly lethargic, her mind too exhausted to cope with the turmoil she knew awaited her in the morning.

CHAPTER NINE

SOMETHING was different. Brooke knew it even
without opening her eyes or admitting returning
consciousness; at first just an awareness that had
been with her as she lay somewhere between
sleeping and waking, her eyes closed, her body
relaxed, now it was a certainty.

Adam ... her mind probed the pleasure even
thinking his name brought and awareness flooded
through her body. There was no regret, only
pleasure mingled with sorrow because by embark-
ing on an affair with Adam, Brooke knew she had
set in motion a chain of events which would
culminate in her losing him.

She moved and became conscious that she was
still in his arms, her fingertips drifted over his
chest, her body coiling achingly. It wasn't yet
dawn and in her naivety she had expected to wake
up exhausted by their lovemaking, but instead
there was this unbelievable sensation of wellbeing,
and a finely tuned and insistent hunger for Adam
that made her want to smile and cry at the same
time.

'Did I hurt you?'

She hadn't realised that Adam was awake and
the abruptness of his stark question halted her
caress.

Honesty and an instinct for self-preservation
warred and then remembering how she had
practically begged him to make love to her Brooke
settled for honesty.

'Not really. . . .' Avoiding his eyes she added candidly, 'I think I'd be aching more if you hadn't made love to me than I am because you did, although in a different way.' Humour tilted the corners of her mouth and because she wasn't looking at him the explosively harsh sound against her ear made her jerk round. Expecting to see laughter she was shocked by the pallor of Adam's skin, and the expression in his eyes. He took her face in his hands, almost bruising her skin with the depth of pressure he was exerting, and her hunger became a raging need.

Compulsively, almost silently, Adam began to make love to her, and Brooke responded, matching him caress for caress following him without hesitation, sometimes awed, sometimes bewildered by the depth of her own sensuality. This time his appetite for her seemed fiercer, keener, and yet less urgent, some of his earlier tension gone. The culmination of their lovemaking came surprisingly quickly, overwhelming her with its wild rush of pleasure.

'There are so many things I want to teach you, show you. . . .' Adam murmured afterwards, caressing her gently into sleep, soothing her with the hypnotic stroke of his hands against her skin.

The next time she woke up it was light and she was alone. Panic, sharp and agonising ripped through her, a bitter foretaste of what the rest of her life was likely to be like, Brooke acknowledged shakily. She couldn't regret what had happened, but where was she going to find the strength now to face the rest of her life without Adam?

The bedroom door opened and he walked in carrying a tray; the sight of him instantly transporting her back to London and another morning . . . her skin paled, her eyes unknowingly shadowed and bruised. She saw his mouth compress and her heart sank.

'Coffee and croissants,' he told her in a clipped voice, putting the tray down beside her. Whereas in the night her nudity had not concerned her at all, now, suddenly she was reluctant to sit up knowing that if she did the sheet would slip. A brief frown scored Adam's forehead and then he leaned down, plucking the shirt he had discarded the previous night, off the floor. 'Here,' he told her tersely, 'put this on.'

He strolled over to the window while she did so, his legs long and bare beneath the hem of his robe. Brooke's heart turned over, her senses betraying her as she caught the male scent of him that clung elusively to his shirt.

'Coffee?' Without waiting for her response Adam poured a generous amount into both cups, adding cream before handing one to her. There was a small parcel on the tray, beautifully packaged and Brooke stared at it as though mesmerised.

'Your Christmas present,' Adam told her softly. 'For some reason I forgot to give it to you last night.'

'Is that why you flew out here?' There was a tight knot of pain in Brooke's voice occasioned by the withdrawal she sensed in him, but sheer dogged necessity forcing her to play his game.

'Yes.' Now his voice was distinctly terse. He was regretting last night already Brooke thought defeatedly, and was probably wondering how on earth he was going to extricate himself from the situation. Well, if he thought she was going to make a fuss he would soon find out that he was wrong. She had known all along that he didn't love her.... Her fingers toyed with the gift wrapping, and Adam's brows drew together in an impatient frown. 'Aren't you going to open it?'

Forcing a wan smile Brooke did so. A small square box emerged from the wrappings, and she frowned, recognising the famous name of the jeweller stamped into the leather. Her querying, hesitant glance meshed with Adam's. 'Open it,' he commanded brusquely. He picked up his own coffee cup, without drinking, watching her so intently that feathers of alarm quivered up and down her spine.

Her fingers trembled as she opened the box, the clasp slightly stiff, the lid flipping back to reveal a perfect emerald ring surrounded by the flashing fire of encircling diamonds.

'Adam ...' her voice was strained and tense. 'I. ... What is this?' she managed at last.

'Your engagement ring.' His voice was cool and remote. 'We're flying back to London this afternoon, and we'll be married at the end of the week. Don't tell me you didn't want to marry me Brooke,' he said quietly, lifting her left hand and kissing the inside of her wrist before he slid the ring on to her finger.

'Why?' She couldn't take it in, couldn't believe what she was hearing.

'It's time I had a wife ... children.... It's what we both want Brooke. You know me well enough to know I never do anything I don't want to do, and I know you well enough to know you wouldn't give yourself lightly.'

'But why me?' She was still dazed; disbelieving.

'Why not?' His glance was wryly mocking. 'Don't underestimate yourself Brooke. You have all the characteristics men value most in their wives. You're loyal, trustworthy, beautiful, chaste. . . .' His tongue lingered over the last word, and Brooke knew unbelievably that it was true, Adam actually wanted to marry her!

'Last night,' she began breathlessly, only to break off as his mouth twisted almost bitterly.

'Not quite what I'd intended. Oh I intended to make love to you all right,' he told her, correctly interpreting her expression, 'but with rather more finesse and rather less fervour. Some things, it seems, cannot be controlled or planned for. You see Brooke when I make plans I like to be sure that they have a good chance of success, and that entails careful groundwork. I wasn't sure if you would marry me, but I knew you wanted me. You realise you could already have conceived our child.'

The heady thrill his soft words brought was quenched by a sudden storm of doubts. Adam had said nothing of love; nothing of feelings, only of 'plans'.

'Adam. . . .'

'No arguments,' he told her curtly. 'Everything's arranged. . . .'

'You were so sure of me?'

'You jump like a nervous fawn every time I come anywhere near you. When I kissed you, the way your body responded to mine, told me you weren't indifferent to me. You've remained a virgin for too long for it to be an accident or a whim. The fact that we're lovers tells me that you feel something for me. I could have waited until after we are married to possess you but then I would never have known what was desire and what was duty. Last night was all desire wasn't it, Brooke?'

Desire and love, she amended mentally, avoiding looking at him. Something was desperately wrong. She should be feeling ecstatically happy but instead she felt apprehensive, full of nervous dread. And yet she knew that if Adam wanted to marrry her, she would do. She was too weak to resist the temptation.

'I'll leave you to get dressed.' He sounded so ridiculously formal that she wanted to laugh, only it was tears that weren't so very far away, not laughter, and suddenly she longed for Adam to take her in his arms and kiss away all her doubts and fears.

They left three hours later, after the LeBruns had returned in time to admire and exclaim over the emerald glowing richly on Brooke's ring finger.

During the flight back Adam appeared pre-occupied and rather than intrude on his thoughts Brooke kept her attention to her small window.

They landed at Heathrow without incident, where a chauffeur-driven car was waiting to meet them.

'I'll drop you off at the apartment,' Adam announced brusquely as they were driven into London. 'I've got several things to attend to, but I shouldn't be gone too long.'

He wasn't gone as long as Brooke had expected, returning as she was unpacking her suitcase in the guest room she had used before. He walked in and leaned up against the wall, studying her almost broodingly, his eyes like ice as he demanded coldly, 'What exactly are you doing?'

'Unpacking my things. Then I thought I'd ring Abbot's Meade, just to make sure that Balsebar is behaving himself.'

'I spoke to Tod on Christmas Eve both dog and

man are doing fine. I can see I'm going to have to
tell that mut that from now on he doesn't come
first in your life.' The look he gave her was so
blazingly possessive that Brooke could feel a surge
of responsive heat deep inside her body, as it
responded to the sexually charged magnetism of
Adam's scrutiny. 'Make no mistake about it
Brooke,' he added still watching her, 'I expect and
intend to be the most important thing in your life
from now on.'

'How very chauvinistic of you.' She said the
words lightly, half turning away from him. This
was a side to Adam she hadn't seen before. He had
meant every carefully chosen word he had said,
and yet he didn't love her.

Her skin prickled warningly as she felt his
proximity. He had moved so quickly and quietly
that she hadn't been aware of it, but now she was
aware of him, deep down in her bones and insides.
His fingers bit tautly into her arm as he swung her
round to face him, and beneath the sardonic
control of his features Brooke sensed a fierce
energy, and something else she couldn't put a
name to.

'I mean it Brooke,' he told her tightly. 'No wife
of mine will ever join the lover swapping circuit so
many of my colleagues' wives embark on.' His
glance was like a whiplash, scoring her skin, so
that she made an involuntary movement to step
away from him, which resulted only in a further
tightening of his grasp. There was pain in the way
his fingers held her and yet there was also an
intense sexual pleasure. Brooke shivered, not sure
if she liked this glimpse of a side of her nature she
hadn't known existed. She wanted to pull away
from Adam, to taunt him until that fine control

she sensed within him was broken and he had no
alternative but to subdue her with his mouth and
body.

She shivered again. 'Subdue,' she tasted the
word a little distastefully. What had happened to
all her dearly held views on marriage and
partnership? Why did she feel this surge of aching
need at the thought of the hungry violence of
Adam's lovemaking? Human responses were never
easy things to understand, she told herself shakily.
Adam had awakened in her a hunger she hadn't
known herself capable of.

'I wonder what's going through your mind
right at this minute?' Adam's softly spoken
question caught her attention. 'You've changed,
Brooke,' he told her. 'When we first met you were
very easy to read, but now you've learned how to
hide your thoughts from me. A gift of your class
of women,' he added derisively. 'Always polite and
charming on the surface, but underneath all too
ready and eager to cheat on their husbands; and
on their lovers.'

What did he mean, 'her class of woman' Brooke
wondered worriedly, shivering again. Did Adam
really think she would cheat on her marriage
vows?

'If women are unfaithful to their husbands, at
least half the time those husbands are to blame,'
she countered, lifting her chin to glare defiantly at
him, and glorying in the sudden glitter of anger
darkening his eyes.

'If you're ever unfaithful to me, I'll. . . .'

'Beat me? Lock me in my room on a diet of
bread and water?' Her voice mocked him, her
excitement growing, pushing her to break through
the barriers of his control. He tensed and Brooke

felt her heart start to thud heavily. He only needed to bend his head to kiss her. She ached for him to do so, but instead he released her, moving slightly away, no sign of anger or any other emotion displayed in his face as he said calmly, 'No, I'd simply make love to you until your body was too sated to even think of another lover.'

He turned and headed for the door, pausing there to throw over his shoulder, 'Which brings me back to what I was going to say originally. What are you doing in here?'

'Unpacking my things,' Brooke repeated looking perplexed.

'In three days' time we're going to be married,' he told her softly. 'I want you in my bed, tonight and every night from now on Brooke.'

'Even though I'm an inexperienced virgin. . . .' She couldn't resist throwing the taunt at him. It was born of a mixture of anguish and self-mockery, because she knew that no matter how much he desired her physically, he had no real emotional feelings for her.

'Were,' he corrected her, his glance sliding insolently over her body. 'And as for your inexperience. . . .' His eyes darkened and Brooke could tell his thoughts had turned inwards. 'Well let's just say that in spite of it, or perhaps because of it, you made me feel like no woman has made me feel in as long as I can remember. Your face doesn't lie when it proclaims you a sensualist, Brooke. Oh, your mind may have subdued those natural urges; you may have resented my sex's reaction to you, but last night fulfilled every promise your face and body has ever made to me, and you enjoyed it as much as I did,' he added before she could speak. 'When I woke up this morning you were still lying in my arms, and when I touched you you responded to me even in your sleep. It's no use trying to lie about it, Brooke,' he added warningly.

'I wasn't going to.' Her body was stiff and tense with pain. 'I was simply going to ask you if you really thought that mere sexual desire was a good grounds for basing a marriage on.'

'Had you been sexually promiscuous, with a long list of lovers to your credit, then no,' he told her frankly, 'because I could never be sure you would stay faithful to me. But I'm your first lover Brooke, and you're fastidious and proud enough to keep the vows you make me.'

'But you ...' Brooke protested, her earlier misgivings returning. This wasn't how they should be entering marriage; 'What will you gain?'

'I've already told you. A woman who feels good in my bed; a charming hostess used to moving in all the right circles, a mother for my children.' He saw the expression on her face and laughed softly. 'Ah yes, that as well Brooke. You want children, don't you?'

'I want your children,' she longed to say, but knew she could not, just as she knew that despite all her misgivings she was going to marry Adam, and somehow that knowledge hurt her pride.

They were married three days later, as Adam had told her. To her surprise the ceremony was a religious and not a civil one, and Adam had arranged a large reception at the Dorchester.

'If it was summer, we could have held the reception at Abbot's Meade,' he told her as they drove towards the Dorchester after the ceremony, 'but the construction work is nowhere near

finished yet and it's far too cold to think of a
marquee in the park.'

Brooke hadn't had time to speak to any of the
guests as they left the church and she felt her
stomach churn with nervousness as she contemplated meeting Adam's friends and business
acquaintances.

'I'm surprised you planned such a large
reception,' she commented, smoothing down the
wild silk fabric of her dress. Adam had insisted on
a traditional wedding dress, although she had
opted for a very pale cream rather than white,
knowing that it suited her complexion and colour
better. It was cut on the simplest of lines and
because she was tall she had been able to get away
with a beautiful spray of cream flowers. There had
been no bridesmaids, mainly because of the
shortage of time, and Tod had been Adam's best
man. Brooke had sensed a slight constraint in Tod
before the ceremony but her anxious queries about
Balsebar had proved unnecessary. The dog was
apparently in excellent health. Pushing aside her
feelings of unease, Brooke folded her hands neatly
in her lap and concentrated on the middle
distance.

It was a trick of composure her mother had
taught her, but for some reason it seemed to annoy
Adam. She could see his mouth tightening as he
turned towards her.

'You look like a martyr going to the flames,' he
told her savagely, shocking her with his bitterness.
He would have said more, she was sure, but they
had reached the Dorchester and the car had
stopped.

The doorman helped them out, and Adam put
his hand under her elbow as he helped Brooke

inside. To an outsider they would probably present a very romantic picture, she thought miserably as they were conducted to their private room.

Everyone else was already assembled, and a bewildering almost frightening sea of unfamiliar faces met Brooke's gaze as the doors were thrown open. At least some of the faces were familiar; she could see Brockbanks, Sam beaming paternally at her; and Tod of course waiting for them on the top table. She could also see Susan Crawford and her heart missed a beat as she saw the cold glitter of a huge diamond ring on the other woman's left hand. At her side stood a small, slightly balding man Brooke didn't recognise, his hand resting proprietorally on Susan's arm.

Adam had obviously followed her gaze, because Brooke saw his mouth tighten as he too looked at the couple and the feeling of misgiving she had had ever since he announced his intention to marry her began to crystallise into a hard knot of fear.

Throughout the meal Brooke tried to smile and appear relaxed, but in fact she was a tightly coiled bundle of nerves. They weren't having a honeymoon because the work at Abbot's Meade had reached a very critical stage and Adam wanted to be there to supervise it. From now on the Dower House would be their permanent home, and although she knew she should have felt pleased, all she could feel was a cold hard lump of misery.

Tod raised his glass to toast them, and Brooke forced another smile. Tod looked almost as worried as she felt. She was pleased to see that all his family had been invited. He had pointed them out to her during the meal. They looked a warm and friendly crowd, unlike the majority of the guests. How many real friends apart from Tod's family, did Adam have, she wondered, studying them. He wasn't a man who gave anything of himself easily, nor would he trust readily, and she knew from what Tod had told her that he bitterly resented the snubs he had been given in the early days of his business career.

At last the ordeal was over—or nearly. The meal had finished and they were now free to wander among their guests. At any normal wedding this would have been a relaxing and pleasurable climax to the day's events, but for her, there was no joy in meeting and being introduced to a long procession of well-fed and almost always overly smug faces.

Only Tod's family seemed real, his mother exclaiming over her dress with genuine pleasure, as she touched the fine fabric. 'Eeh but that's a lovely bit of material,' she commented; adding to one of her daughters, 'Look, our Sylvia, you should get something like this when you marry young Terry.'

'Chance 'ud be a fine thing,' Sylvia commented with a lively grin in Brooke's direction. 'It's silk, Ma, and it costs a small fortune. Besides,' she added with a practicality that warmed Brooke's bruised heart, 'even if we could afford it, I'd sooner the money was spent on the house.'

Adam moved away to speak to someone else, and Brooke thankfully sat down in the chair Tod's mother pulled out for her.

'So our Adam's got himself wed at last,' she commented, studying her. 'Well there's no doubt about it, you're a right bonny lass, but looks aren't everything, and our Tod says you've got a lovely nature as well.' She glanced lovingly at her son, who grimaced and looked faintly embarrassed. 'We're all right glad Adam didn't go and wed that toffee-nosed Susan. Too good for him she thought herself, but not good enough by a long chalk, that's what I say.'

'Ma. . . .' Tod's voice had a warning note in it, and Brooke tensed, worried by the look exchanged by mother and son, but Adam had returned and was patiently waiting for her to re-join him.

They were three-quarters of the way round the room before Brooke found the courage to ask a question. 'Adam, how many of these people are your real friends?'

'You mean how many of them accept me as I am; how many of them would still be here, if I wasn't Adam Henderson Hart of Hart Enterprises?' he asked grimly. 'What's the matter? Are you worried that you won't get enough acceptances to your invitations to fill your dinner table? Are you worried about being ashamed of me Brooke; of having to face the snide comments and mockery of your social peers? Well you should have thought about that before.' Almost savagely he released her arm and strode away from her, leaving Brooke shocked by his outburst. Tod had warned her that Adam still retained the bitter memories of his childhood, but she had had no idea that they were so deep-rooted or vitriolic. Frowning she turned away, only to be accosted by Susan and her escort.

'Darling, do go and get me another drink would you,' she trilled sweetly. 'Trust Adam to serve the very best champagne. Vulgar of course . . . but then what else can one expect.'

When her escort had gone to do her bidding she smiled mockingly at Brooke. 'Well, well, so Adam finally did it.'

Grimly telling herself that she wasn't going to

give the blonde the satisfaction of asking the obvious question Brooke turned away. 'He always said he would, but I didn't think anyone would ever be stupid enough to go along with him, but then I suppose in your circumstances it was either Adam or some dreary accountant. I suppose you expect that the combination of your family background and his money . . .' she broke off, and smiled secretly, much to Brooke's fury. 'Of course I always knew that Adam would stop at nothing to get himself socially accepted, but you?' Her eyebrows arched. 'Of course you know that he asked *me* to marry him?' Her unkind laughter filled Brooke's ears, breaking through her pain.

'Daddy was furious, although of course, he couldn't say much about it because of this deal he's involved in with Adam. Naturally I refused him.' She glanced complacently at the diamond glittering on her left hand, in its own way as vulgar as she had called Adam's champagne, Brooke thought fiercely. 'I had to tell him when he proposed to me that I'd already accepted Leon. Not that it would have made any difference. My set would have shunned me completely, if I had married him. There are some things money just can't compensate for. Oh Adam's done extremely well for himself, and in bed. . . .' Her eyebrows arched delicately, her small pink tongue touching her lips in a way that made Brooke long to rake her nails down her face, the intensity of her emotions making her feel almost sick. 'But as a husband! I suppose of course, he told you he loved you? It's your family background he loves my dear. He's never made any secret of the fact that he intended to marry well, and he won't be a faithful husband.'

'Just as you won't be a faithful wife,' Brooke broke in too angry to care what she was saying. A sick, despairing feeling flooded through her. Knowing what she did about Adam's background it was all too easy to believe what Susan was saying. She was perhaps the only woman he had ever loved, and she had embittered him to the extent where he was capable of marrying for exactly those reasons she had described. But it had come as a shock to hear that he had proposed to her so recently. He must have made up his mind to marry her almost immediately afterwards, and that was why everything had been arranged with such haste. Even making love to her had probably been calculated and planned, she thought bitterly. He must have known that once they had been lovers she would be more inclined to marry him. The desperate passion and hunger she had sensed in him had not been for her after all, they had been the result of his rejection by Susan.

'Brooke?'

Tod was standing beside her, looking concerned. Susan had gone and how long she had been standing alone Brooke did not know. 'You look pale,' he told her, 'are you okay?'

'Fine. It's just been a long day.'

'Soon be over now. Brooke. . . .' He frowned and glanced uncertainly at his hands, square, capable hands Brooke noticed absently.

'Brooke, don't take this the wrong way, but do you love Adam?'

'Does it matter?' her voice ached with raw pain. 'I know why he married me Tod, if that's what's worrying you.' She broke away before Tod could say anything else, pain and bitter anguish tearing into her like cruelly sharp spurs. Adam had deceived her; he hadn't had the honesty to tell her why he was marrying her. He had guessed how she felt about him and he had used her feelings quite callously to get what he wanted; to show Susan that even if she rejected him, others would not.

Now she understood the reason for the lavish reception, and the impressive guest list, and her heart ached anew; both for herself and for Adam. Surely he could see that he was pursuing a chimera; that the so called 'acceptance' of those people who could be impressed by wealth and power simply wasn't worth having. And she couldn't help him. She had never mixed in the glossy superficial circles favoured by Susan and her like and she shrank from doing so.

'Brooke.'

Adam's sharp voice intruded on her misery. 'Isn't it time you got changed?'

'I'm on my way.' She turned away from him as she spoke not wanting him to see the pain and misery in her eyes. She was a substitute for Susan Crawford. Adam didn't even want her physically for herself, but for what she represented. Despite the centrally heated room set on one side for her to change in she was shivering convulsively as she slid out of her wedding dress and into the chestnut wool dress she had chosen to return to Abbot's Meade in.

CHAPTER TEN

BROOKE could never remember travelling back to Abbot's Meade in such acute misery in her whole life.

Adam made desultory conversation as he drove, to which she responded with what she knew to be lacklustre and stilted monosyllables, but despite all the urgings of her pride she couldn't find the willpower to sound happy and unconcerned.

She had known he didn't love her—at least not as she loved him—and she had been able to come to terms with that, but this new discovery was too soon and too devastating for her to cope with. Their marriage was destroyed before it had even really started she thought weakly. Another stronger woman might have been able to fight; to play a game of 'let's pretend' in the hope that eventually their sham relationship might be transformed into a real one, but Brooke was beyond any form of pretence, never mind such a sophisticated one. And it didn't help knowing that she was a fool for not seeing the truth for herself. But it was too late to berate herself now. She and Adam were married; they had been lovers. A wave of nausea wrenched through her, leaving her pale and aching with pain. How could she endure having him touch her again now that she knew the truth? She couldn't adopt the cynical attitudes of a woman like Susan.

'Are you all right?' The curt question whipped

across her lacerated nerves, sending acute waves of pain shuddering through her nervous system.

'Brooke?'

The harsh utterance of her name made her tremble, and yet why should she be so afraid, Adam knew nothing of her decision yet.

She wasn't going to sleep with him, she decided frantically, she could not. He would have to take whatever steps he wished to end their marriage. A strangled noise issued from her throat causing Adam to switch his attention from his driving to her.

'Too much champagne,' he derided, mockingly. 'Lie back and close your eyes.'

Brooke did as he directed, more from a need to escape the cool, too-knowing scrutiny of his eyes than because she wanted to. Adam was astute and she was frightened that he would read her anguish in her eyes. She wasn't afraid of telling him of her decision, but she wanted to do it with a little more courage and self-control than she was capable of just now.

When they turned into Abbot's Meade's drive, the house loomed large and dark ahead of them. Adam swung his car expertly round towards the Dower House. Smoke curled out of the chimneys, lights glowing behind the curtains. As though anticipating her question Adam murmured, 'I arranged for someone to come in and organise fires and food.' His eyes went to the thin curl of smoke. 'It looks very inviting, doesn't it, but like everything else, looks aren't everything. When I was a boy my mother used to have to go scavenging along at the back of the local railway yard to get coal—stealing it, really if we're being honest, but if she didn't come home with any we didn't have a fire, and the walls in our terraced house ran with damp during the winter. My mother suffered from severe arthritis towards the end of her life. . . .'

It was the first time he had mentioned anything personal from his past to her, and in other circumstances Brooke would have been brought to the edge of sympathetic tears by his casual disclosures, but now all she could feel was a dull numbness, a disinterest that manifested itself in her slow turning of her head to stare out of the window, leaving his remarks uncommented upon.

'Sorry about that.' His voice grated roughly against her ears, and had she not so recently learned how hard he could be she might almost have supposed it to contain pain. 'Obviously, you aren't interested in the sordid details of my childhood. I'll make note not to mention them again. Worrying you is it; how you're going to endure the social solecisms of your lower-class husband. . . .'

This was it. Brooke took a deep breath and held it, it was now or never; she must tell him while she could.

'Not really.' She was proud of her cool, distant voice that didn't tremble or betray any shade of emotion whatsoever. 'You see, Adam, I made a mistake. I don't want to be married to you after all.'

The silence in the car pressed heavily down on her. She daren't look into Adam's face, and then without saying a word to her he opened the car door and got out. When he opened her door Brooke fought down panic. His face was impassive; she could read nothing in it.

Perhaps he thought she was suffering from

bridal nerves she thought feverishly. If so she
would have to convince him that she was serious,
although he would know that the moment he
touched her. Her blood actually seemed to run
cold at the thought of him touching any part of
her body, no matter how casually. It was the deep
intensity of her love for him that had caused this
bitter revulsion, she acknowledged; and it was
directed as much against herself as against him.
She had enjoyed his lovemaking; if a word such as
'enjoy' could describe the wealth of sensation and
pleasure he had given her, and now her mind was
punishing her body for that enjoyment; for putting
it in a position where it could be humiliated in this
way. She still loved him; that was the most
incredible thing of all; and yet she hated him at the
same time; and she hated herself.

His fingers reached for her arm to help her out
of the car and she froze, watching the expression
on his face, as though she were a complete
outsider to the small drama, watching herself.
Anger, deep and penetrating, set his face into
harsh lines, his mouth thinning as he withdrew and
went to open the boot.

Following him inside, Brooke shivered, despite
the enveloping heat of the centrally heated hall.

Part of her mind recognised that a small army
must have been at work in the Dower House since
she left it because not only had discreetly hidden
central heating been installed, but the hall had
been restored to its original glory, the mouldings
and plasterwork delicately picked out in white,
against the soft peach of the walls. A thick, plain
pearl grey carpet muffled their footsteps, and
flowed up the sweeping staircase.

'In here.'

Adam's voice was curt as he thrust open the door to the drawing room. Here again the floor was covered in the pearl grey carpet. The walls had been painted in a soft yellow with an attractive stippled effect, the plasterwork once again white.

Two large, comfortable settees upholstered in an attractive yellow, French blue and soft grey traditional fabric were positioned either side of the Adam fireplace, an elegant coffee table in between them.

A Regency writing desk and several other attractive antiques of the same period added warmth to the room, and Brooke knew that this was somewhere she could have felt at home in. It was an attractive room, elegant and yet comfortable.

'Sit down and I'll get us both a drink.'

'I don't want one.' How stiff and formal her voice sounded.

'Maybe not, but I do.'

She sank down on to one of the settees, her hands folded primly in her lap, tension infusing every part of her body. Behind her she could hear Adam pouring his drink and the tension grew.

'Now,' he said tersely, when he came to stand in front of her, 'would you mind explaining to me exactly what you meant out there in the car.'

'Exactly what I said,' Brooke told him bravely. 'I've changed my mind, Adam, I don't want to be married to you.'

'After less than five hours of marriage, you've decided you don't want it, is that it? I was good enough as your lover, but not as your husband.' His face contorted with a mixture of emotions she couldn't define, as he tilted his glass and drank the contents in one swallow. 'And to think I thought you were different—warm and human....' He grimaced with disgust and Brooke had to stop herself from screaming at him that he was the one who was cold and without emotion; he was the one who had married her because.... Her mind shied away, still not wholly ready to accept the truth.

'Well, I'll just have to see if I can't change your mind, won't I?'

Before she knew what was happening she was in Adam's arms and he was carrying her towards the stairs. Struggling frantically to escape, Brooke glared up at his impassive face. Despite her height he didn't need to check as he carried her upstairs, and shock began to give way to fear.

'Adam....'

'Save your breath, Brooke,' he told her tersely, thrusting open a door with his shoulder. The room beyond lay in shadow, dominated by the bulk of a large half-tester bed. A fire had been lit in the grate, the flames flickering shadows round the walls, highlighting the soft muted shades of peach and cream in which the room was decorated.

The bed sank beneath her weight as Adam dropped her on it. Brooke reacted instinctively, twisting to one side, rolling desperately away intent on escape, but Adam foiled her, pinning her to the bed by straddling her body, gripping it with his knees as he used his hands to pull off her jacket.

Brooke was a tall girl, and she had always thought a fairly strong one, but despite her angry struggles Adam easily overpowered her.

When his hands reached the waistband of her skirt she tensed in furious protest, hating him with her eyes, loathing the touch of his fingers against her skin.

'It's coming off Brooke,' he responded thickly. 'I'll tear it off you if I have to.'

He did, and the harsh noise of the tearing fabric was like a cry of anguish for all that their marriage could have been and was not.

Brooke lay motionless, cold as marble as he removed the rest of her clothes and then his own. She was beyond any thought of escape, beyond anything but keeping herself from being acutely sick. Even Adam's driving anger didn't have the power to touch her. He didn't kiss her, simply staring broodingly down at her before gripping her shoulders and then slowly sliding his hands down her body until he was cupping her breasts. Unable to tear her eyes away from the sight of his tanned fingers against her skin Brooke felt a wave of nausea rise up inside her.

In a voice completely devoid of any trace of feeling she said quietly, 'Adam if you don't stop touching me, I'm afraid I shall be sick.'

He withdrew almost immediately, and for a moment it seemed that his skin was almost grey, his eyes winter bleak.

'Why?' he asked in a voice that matched her own for emptiness.

'Because I know the truth.' What was the point in hiding it; he might as well know. 'I know why you married me.'

This time he really did lose colour. For a moment his eyes blazed down at her and then they were masked, his emotions banked down.

'And because of that you can't bear me to touch you?'

'If I'd known before I'd never have married you,' she told him quietly, 'and now that I do know, I can't stay married to you.'

'I see.'

He moved slowly into the shadows of the room, withdrawing from the bed.

'Well, there doesn't seem to be much else to say does there? I thought we might be able to work it out—we both have something to give each other, but I can see I hadn't taken everything into account. I think it's probably best if I return to London—at least until we sort out what's going to happen.'

'This is your home,' Brooke protested, feeling guilty in spite of herself. 'I'll leave. I'll go back to the Lodge.' With a pang she realised that she would have to sell the Lodge now; she couldn't continue to live there after this. She would have to look for a new job as well, she realised on a sudden flood of near hysteria.

'I have others.' He pulled on his clothes, and Brooke watched him, unable to stop herself from admiring the fluid lines of his body, but the thought of that body against hers still made her shudder with self-loathing.

Of course, she couldn't sleep, not even after she had heard Adam drive away. She was up early, wandering aimlessly from room to room of the newly restored Dower House. In other circumstances she knew she would have loved living in it, but right now.... Nothing felt real; she seemed to have wandered into a nightmare world where she cringed away from contact with everything.

Long walks with Balsebar did little to ease her tension. A week went by and she had still heard nothing from Adam. She went into town and arranged for the Lodge to be put up for sale.

There was no point in delaying things, it wouldn't serve any useful purpose.

Ten days after her wedding day it snowed; a crisp white blanket that lay a couple of inches deep over the countryside, and seeing it seemed to break through the ice in which she had encased herself. Brooke found herself crying painfully, suddenly and excruciatingly vulnerable to all the emotions she had held at bay so far.

Her crying jag left her with an aching head and sore eyes which she was bathing with cold water when she heard the front door bell. Her heart leapt, but it wasn't Adam at the door, but Tod.

He looked worriedly at her as she let him in, bending absently to pat Balsebar's black head.

'So you *are* here,' he said abruptly as he followed her into the drawing room. 'I thought you might be. Look,' he added, without preamble, 'I don't know what's gone wrong between you and Adam but it's tearing him apart. . . .'

'The man with the computer brain?' Brooke derided.

Tod looked shocked. 'Is that what you think? You haven't seen him recently. He's destroying himself, Brooke; working all hours God sends and then going back to that apartment of his to drink and. . . .'

'Drink?'

Tod's mouth twisted derisively, 'Why so surprised, isn't it the traditional escape-route from pain for men who lose the woman they love.'

He saw her blench and stepped forward, to catch her as she swayed. 'Look,' he said roughly, 'I don't know what's gone wrong between the pair of you, but it's obvious that you're crazily in love with one another. . . .'

'I might be in love with Adam, but he certainly isn't with me,' Brooke interrupted recklessly. 'He still loves Susan, I'm just a substitute. . . .'

'He told you that?' Tod sounded disbelieving.

'No, but she did, and it all adds up when you really think about it. You said yourself that Adam had a chip on his shoulder because she hurt his pride. . . .'

'Adam loves you.' He sounded positive. 'I'm sure of it Brooke,' he insisted. 'Oh at first, I didn't think so, but after seeing him for these last ten days. . . . He's destroying himself,' he told her softly, 'if you don't believe me, go and see for yourself.'

She wanted to refuse, but it was too late, hope had already taken a firm root in her heart. Could she have been wrong? She desperately wanted to believe that she might have been ... too desperately, she cautioned herself, but Tod wasn't giving her time to think.

'Come back with me now,' he insisted. 'I'll drive you up to London. Go and see Adam, talk to him openly and honestly. . . .'

'He's never said anything about loving me. . . .'

'Have you ever told him how you feel about him?' Tod countered. 'Yes, long ago Susan did hurt him and because of it, he's learned to hide his feelings, but he wouldn't have married you if he hadn't loved you Brooke.'

'Not even to gain the right sort of wife?' she asked grimacing.

'Go and see him,' Tod urged. 'He needs you Brooke.'

It was a plea she knew she couldn't resist. Leaving Tod with Balsebar she hurried upstairs, quickly flinging clothes into a small case, her heart hammering with nervous excitement and relief.

Suddenly, gloriously she was free of the dark spell Susan had woven round her; suddenly she could remember how she had felt in Adam's arms; how much she wanted him; her body pulsed hungrily and all at once she ached for the physical act of his possession. Colour swept up under her skin, and she laughed at herself in her mirror, deriding her reflection, half-amused and half-ashamed of the sudden surge of feeling taking over her body.

'I'll have to drop you here,' Tod apologised, stopping outside the apartment block. 'I can't get into the car park because I don't have a pass.' He leaned across her to open her door, and whispered, 'Good luck.' Brooke smiled hesitantly back at him. Now that she was here, so close to Adam, she was beginning to have second thoughts. How could she face him? How would he react to her? Did he really care about her, or was Tod wrong?'

'Isn't he worth fighting for,' Tod asked softly watching her. 'He's a proud man Brooke, and I'm not promising that it will be easy. . . .'

'No. . . .' She sighed and straightened her shoulders, as she got out of the car walking quickly towards the door and into the foyer.

It was completely deserted as she rang the bell for the lift. It carried her smoothly upwards and then stopped.

As Brooke stepped out, a cloud of butterflies beat their wings stormily inside her stomach. Almost as though fate had decided to give her a helping hand Adam's door was slightly open. She pushed it and walked in, curling her fingers into her palms as she tried to control her nervousness.

As she stepped into the living room the carpet muffled the sound of her footsteps.

Adam was standing in the middle of the room, but he wasn't alone. Susan was with him. Not just with him Brooke thought bitterly but in his arms, both of them too involved with one another to even notice her arrival.

So much for Tod's claim that Adam loved her, she thought achingly, turning to go, shocked by the sudden rush of betraying tears stinging her eyes.

'Brooke.'

She froze as she heard Adam's imperative command, and then turned her head in obedience to it. His face looked pale, his eyes very dark and slightly sunken, throwing his cheek bones into prominence. A smear of Susan's lipstick smudged his mouth, the sight of it too much for Brooke's shattered self-control. Deliberately breaking contact with Adam's eyes, she turned away, ignoring his fierce demand for her to stay.

The lift was there, as she had left it and she plunged wildly into it, pressing the button. The doors closed just as Adam reached them; anger, bitterness, etched into his face as he stared at her.

She took that image of him back to Abbot's Meade with her. The phone was ringing as she walked in but she ignored it, calmly gathering up her clothes and collecting Balsebar. She couldn't spend another night in the Dower House; she couldn't lie in the bed which had obviously been intended for both of them, picturing Adam with Susan.

Suddenly she wanted to be violently ill. She reached the bathroom just in time, emerging white-faced and grim. This sickness was a new thing for her, brought on she had thought by nerves and anguish, but what if there was another reason? That would be the final irony she thought grimly; to have conceived Adam's child in those few nights they had spent together.

She had no energy left to worry about that possibility now. All she wanted to do was to escape from this house.

The Lodge was cold and musty. Balsebar whined pathetically while she lit the fire, making it plain that he didn't exactly care for this sudden change of lifestyle.

'Too bad,' she told him unfeelingly, pushing him away from the hearth.

An icy coldness had invaded her body; a pain which she had tried to lock away and couldn't hide from any longer. Adam and Susan. Adam. . . . She shivered and then tensed as she heard footsteps outside the house. She had locked the front door when she came in. The bell rang and she waited, refusing to move. The sound died away and so did the retreating footsteps. Her reaction had been an illogical one, but right now she couldn't cope with anyone else, it was as much as she could do to cope with herself.

In the kitchen Balsebar barked and then fell silent but she remained where she was, kneeling in front of the fire. Something damp dropped on to her knee soaking through the fine wool of her skirt. Wondering she examined it and then touched her face. She was crying, and yet she hadn't known it. From now on her life would be pain.

'Brooke?'

She turned round to face the door, her eyes rounding with disbelief. Adam stood there.

'The back door was unlocked,' he told her grimly as she glanced past him into the kitchen.

'Anyone could have walked in here and found you,' he added, making her shiver with the intensity of his anger.

'At least they would have found me *alone*.'

She could have bitten her tongue out for that comment, but it was too late. Adam dropped to his knees next to her, grasping her chin, turning her to face him.

'Why are you crying?' he asked abruptly, 'And why did you come to see me this evening?'

'I wanted to talk to you about our divorce.'

'Does that answer both questions?'

Something about him had changed, Brooke couldn't tell what it was, but she sensed an elation about him at variance with the grimness of his expression and her heart dropped heavily in pain. Had Susan changed her mind; broken off her engagement so that. . . . Her thoughts churned to a chaotic muddle as Adam gently touched her damp face with his fingers.

'You look pale, and you've lost more weight.'

'I could say the same thing about you.'

'Perhaps we're both suffering from the same malady.' He said it casually but it came too close to what Tod had told her and the hopeless joy she had felt afterwards for her to be able to bear it with equanimity. Fresh tears welled and fell. She tried to pull away, telling herself that it was undignified and offensive for a woman of her age and height to dissolve into tears like a baby, but Adam wouldn't release her. His fingers slid along her jaw and into her hair, smoothing the strands almost tenderly away from her face.

'Tell me again why you don't want to be married to me?' he demanded watching her. His fingers winding through her hair stopped her from moving away and she swallowed tensely. 'You know why. . . . Because I know the truth. . . .'

'What truth?'

Unbelievably, he was smiling faintly, his eyes registering the betraying rapidity of the pulse in her throat. He touched it gently with one finger, trailing it upwards along her jaw, tracing the outline of her mouth almost lazily as he watched her.

How could he do this so soon after she had seen him with Susan in his arms, and why?

'What truth, Brooke?' His finger ceased tormenting her vulnerable mouth, but just as she drew in a faint sigh of relief he bent his head, capturing her parted lips and caressing them with his mouth, kissing her with a slow seductiveness that turned her whole body fluid. The sheer unexpectedness of it alone was enough to overwhelm her starved senses. Her lips softened and clung, wanting, needing the touch of his, her eyes closing as she trembled with the tidal flood of aching hunger pouring through her.

'Please. . . .' She managed to pull away from him. 'Please don't do that.'

'Why, because it makes you sick?'

The words were calm, almost thoughtful but they jerked Brooke back into awareness.

'I don't know why you're doing this, Adam,' she said painfully, 'what game you're playing, but I won't be used as a substitute for Susan.'

'Who told you you could ever be that?'

The sheer cruelty of the careless words murmured almost absently made her ache and grit her teeth, determined not to let him see the damage he had done.

'Susan did,' she responded huskily. 'She told me

why you married me Adam. Did you come here
tonight to tell me that she's changed her mind;
that she wants you after all?'

'She's always wanted me.' A smile tugged at the
corners of Adam's mouth and Brooke stared at
him incredulously, before shock gave way to
reality.

'As a lover, yes,' she agreed. 'I'm talking about
wanting you as a husband.'

'I'm married to you,' he reminded her avoiding
the question. 'Tod rang me.'

He added on the last three words thoughtfully,
and Brooke realised that he was watching her. Her
whole body started to tremble. Dear God surely
Tod hadn't told him. . . .

'He's been very concerned about you.' How
banal the words sounded.

'Has he? He didn't sound it. He wanted to know
what I'd been doing to make you so unhappy.
That's something I haven't stopped asking myself
since the day we got married, but tonight's the first
time I've come anywhere near knowing the
answer.

'Do you remember what I said to you the first
time you came here?'

The sudden abrupt change of subject startled
her. 'You told me you weren't interested in
virgins.' Brooke responded drily.

'Not per se,' he agreed, getting to his feet, and
looking down at her. 'I'm beginning to think that
was when I made my first big mistake.'

To Brooke's surprise he bent down and picked
her up.

'Adam. . . .'

Her protest was ignored as he moved determinedly towards the stairs.

'Adam, put me down,' she demanded urgently as he thrust open her bedroom door.

'As Madame wishes.' He was smiling at her as he deposited her on the bed.

Brooke couldn't understand what was going on; why Adam was here or what purpose he had in mind. She stared at him as he calmly started to undress, unable to believe her eyes. Only when he moved towards the bed was she galvanised into action, too late to avoid the firm hands quickly stripping her body of its covering, in direct contradiction of all her heated protests.

'Now. . . .' Something warm and tender glinted in his eyes as he looked down at her, his fingers curling round her upper arms. 'I'm beginning to think I've wasted a hell of a lot of time and caused us both untold misery by not listening to my instincts first time round.'

Brooke tensed as he lifted her, holding her in his arms as he sat down on her bed. Her fingers clutched at his shoulders for support as he lay down, taking her with him, holding her against his body. Its heat and strength seemed to envelop her, sapping her will. She could feel her tense muscles relaxing, her skin soothed by the intimate contact with his.

'The very first time I saw you I wanted to make love to you, but I knew it would be dangerous.' He was tracing tiny kisses along her cheek bone and Brooke had to fight to listen to what he was saying. 'I thought I could resist the temptation, but I was only deceiving myself.'

'You wanted me so much that when I was staying at your apartment you sent me away.' Brooke reminded him, forcing herself to remember all the anguish he had caused her, trying to ignore

the seductive stroke of his fingers against her skin
and the growing heat of their combined need.

'The last dying throes of the male animal
fighting for freedom,' Adam mocked. 'I came after
you, didn't I?' he whispered against her mouth,
feathering it lightly with his own until her lips
became soft and moist clinging to his and then
opening beneath them.

His kiss was leisurely, seductive, and unhurried,
teasing and tantalising until Brooke's tongue
probed exploratively between the hard warmth of
his lips. He groaned deep in his throat, the sound
primitive and exciting, his hands urgent as they
moved over her, and she melted under the impact
of his mouth.

'Because Susan had refused you,' Brooke
murmured painfully when he had released her.
How could she think sensibly when he was
assaulting her defences so skilfully. Her body cried
out for him, demanding that she ignore the
warnings of her mind.

'Susan never had the chance to refuse me,' he
derided, stunning her. 'Come on Brooke,' he
added tautly. 'Do you really think I would want a
woman like her as my wife? She's avaricious and
vain, shallow to an extent that almost defies
imagination.'

'You loved her.' Her voice broke over the
words.

'I was infatuated with her once, when I was little
more than a boy. She hurt me badly, it's true, but
it was my pride she left raw, not my heart. I've
never loved her; and certainly did not marry you
because I couldn't have her.'

He was nibbling her throat, dizzying her
senses, seducing her away from reason. Her

fingertips trembled against his chest and she felt the sudden urgent tension in his body as she touched him. He wanted her; that at least was real.

'Why didn't you say something then, the night of our wedding, when I told you that I knew the truth?'

Somehow Brooke managed to gasp out the words despite her body's response to him.

'Because I thought we were discussing a different truth.'

His words puzzled Brooke and she drew away slightly so that she could look into his face. It looked guarded and yet curiously vulnerable.

'What truth?'

'This truth.'

He said it quietly, drawing her back into his arms and kissing her with a hungry, aching urgency that made her senses sing and her body cling to the shuddering heat of his.

'I thought you'd guessed that I love you,' he muttered against her ear. 'I thought you couldn't bear to touch me because you didn't want that love. Those few words destroyed weeks of careful plotting and scheming. You see I was so sure that you must feel something for me. You responded to me sexually so intensely that I couldn't believe it was merely physical desire. I'd hoped that once we were married those feelings would grow into love. I knew you didn't trust me, and I couldn't endure the trauma of a long courtship; always worrying about losing you. That was why I made love to you in France.'

'That was the only reason?' Brooke arched her eyebrows, suddenly deliriously confident enough to tease him a little. As he looked back at her, she laughed softly and pressed her lips against his throat.

'There were other considerations.' His voice was wryly self-mocking. 'I knew in London how I felt about you, but I wasn't ready to admit then that I loved you to the point where nothing else mattered. That came later, when I'd sent you away. I'd fought against loving you from the moment I saw you, and then suddenly I stopped fighting. I was terrified you'd slip away. I had to make sure of you. . . . You didn't love me, but you wanted me. . . . Yes you did,' he drawled when she opened her mouth to object. 'I thought if I could get you to commit yourself to me sexually. . . .'

'You could force me into marrying you,' Brooke said for him.

'Love can grow.'

'And you were prepared to wait?'

'I was, but I don't have to do I?' he murmured against her skin. 'Tod told me that you love me.'

Brooke didn't say anything.

'Brooke?'

The emotions burning in his eyes as he grated her name thrilled her. All that she had dreamed of seeing was there, laid bare to her gaze, and her heart almost literally turned over in wondering response.

'Almost from the very start,' she admitted, 'but like you I fought against it. I thought I was just to be another sexual conquest, and then when you proposed I hoped, like you, that you might come to feel something for me other than mere sexual desire, but Susan destroyed those hopes.'

'That bitch.' Adam added something uncomplimentary under his breath.

'She was in your apartment, when I came to see

you,' Brooke reminded him. 'You were kissing her.'

'She was kissing *me* as it happens. She'd come round on the pretext of bringing some papers from her father. She leaves me completely cold Brooke, and when you saw us I was simply pushing her away.'

She believed him, just as she now believed that he loved her.

'Tod rang just after I had managed to get rid of her. I was furious with him for delaying me coming after you, but when I heard what he'd got to say, I couldn't believe what I was hearing. He asked if you'd arrived safely, and when I said you'd left again he let me have a few very uncomplimentary home-truths. That very first time at Abbot's Meade, I pictured you like this, in my arms, your body warming mine. If I'd followed my instincts and made love to you then neither of us need have suffered any of this anguish.'

Brooke sighed and moved restlessly against him, concealing a wicked smile.

'Are we going to spend all night talking?' she complained mock peevishly, 'because if we are. . . .'

'Had you something else in mind?' Adam's voice was light, but Brooke had a sudden memory of the urgency of his lovemaking; of the way he had hungered for and responded to her touch, and with the confidence that came from knowing she was loved, she reached out and touched him, kissing his skin lightly, stroking it with her fingers, teasing him, until his fingers covered hers, his breathing short and laboured.

'Brooke!' The way he said her name was a plea and a demand, his body tense as he pulled her against it, his voice ragged and almost unfamiliar as he muttered words of love and need against her skin, and all games-playing was forgotten, submerged by the powerful surge of response dominating her body.

'Tell me you love me.'

Half-mesmerised by the touch of his hands, bemused by the need in his voice, Brooke did and was glad she had made the small sacrifice when she heard him respond, 'And I love you Brooke; so much that I don't know if I can find the words.' He bent his head covering her mouth with his own in passionate demand, and as she responded eagerly to him Brooke knew that the words weren't necessary. The way he held her, the way he kissed and touched her, said it all.

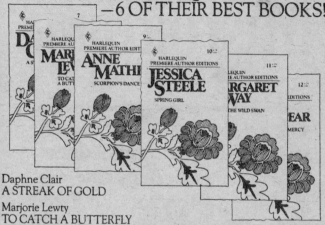

Harlequin reaches
into the hearts and minds
of women across America
to bring you

Harlequin American Romance™

YOURS FREE!

Get this book FREE!

Mail to:
Harlequin Reader Service

In the U.S.	In Canada
2504 West Southern Ave.	P.O. Box 2800, Postal Station A
Tempe, AZ 85282	5170 Yonge St., Willowdale, Ont. M2N 5T5

YES! I want to be one of the first to discover
Harlequin American Romance. Send me FREE and without
obligation *Twice in a Lifetime.* If you do not hear from me after I
have examined my FREE book, please send me the 4 new
Harlequin American Romances each month as soon as they
come off the presses. I understand that I will be billed only $2.25
for each book (total $9.00). There are no shipping or handling
charges. There is no minimum number of books that I have to
purchase. In fact, I may cancel this arrangement at any time.
Twice in a Lifetime is mine to keep as a FREE gift, even if I do not
buy any additional books. **154 BPA NAZJ**

Name   (please print)

Address   Apt. no.

City   State/Prov.   Zip/Postal Code

Signature (If under 18, parent or guardian must sign.)